KENNEDY DEVEREAUX

THE DEVEREAUX FAMILY SERIES

BERNADETTE MARIE

5 PRINCE PUBLISHING

Published by 5 PRINCE PUBLISHING & BOOKS, LLC

PO Box 865, Arvada, CO 80001

www.5PrinceBooks.com

ISBN digital: 978-1-63112-252-1

ISBN print: 978-1-63112-253-8

Cover Credit: Marianne Nowicki

To Stan,
Thank you for supporting and
embracing my obsession with pink,
and its powerful message of being a strong woman.
I know it's not always easy to put up with.
I love you!

ACKNOWLEDGMENTS

To the five that give me insight into how brothers act to one another, I love you all, and your compassion for each other—even if you're knocking one another over.

To Mom and Sissy, we are a dynamic trio—a force that can't be stopped. Feminine and fabulous. I dare anyone to try to take us down now.

To Dad, "Doubt her, then watch her." Thanks for the motto.

To Cate, You make me shine, girlfriend! I appreciate you more than you could ever know.

To Sally G., You brought boutiques like Kennedy's into my life, and I have drawn on that to create her store. I loved that house when you showed clothes and when I had my own business there. You were a powerful woman of the 80's and 90's, and I loved watching you work in your element. Thank you for those memories.

To my Book Hive, Street Team, and Readers, Thank you for embracing the families I create. I fall in love with them as much as you do, and your kind words make me keep wanting to create.

BERNADETTE MARIE

KENNEDY DEVEREAUX

CHAPTER 1

*P*ink doors, crystal light fixtures, white shelves. Joel cupped his hands around his eyes to get a better look at the feminine interior of the store he stood in front of. *Kennedy Devereaux Designs*, the lettering on the door said. Costume jewelry, purses, and a few pieces of clothing were elegantly displayed on uncluttered shelves. He could see a small sitting area toward the back of the store with white chairs on a plush pink rug.

When he stepped back from the door, he inhaled. Could he even smell the store and all of its femininity?

"Can I help you?" A soft voice had him turning to see a woman, as feminine as the store, standing behind him.

She was the smell—sweet and floral. Soft golden hair framed a delicate face, and her lipstick matched the soft pastel pink of the doors he'd been looking through. Sharp blue eyes watched him as he stared at her.

Joel Kingsley was no idiot around women, but this one seemed to render him speechless.

"We don't open for an hour, but if you're looking for something specific, I could help you with that," she said as if to wake him from the trance that he'd fallen into.

"Sorry," he said, tucking his fingers into the front pockets of his jeans. "I was just looking in the window. New to the neighborhood and wanted to check out who else was here."

"New to the neighborhood? You just moved in?"

Joel nodded to the building next door. "New business neighbor."

The woman looked past him to the old building which had once been the post office, then was broken down into retail businesses. They were about to reopen the space and make it grand again.

"You're putting a business in the building next door? Which part?"

"All of it," he said rocking back on his heels. "We're gutting it and starting fresh. When we pulled back the dry wall on the north wall, we even uncovered all the old mailboxes. They'd just walled them up."

Her eyes were wide. "You'll be doing a lot of construction?"

"Of course. Ideally now is when we'd like to be opening. Spring and summer are great times for this kind of business. But permits took a lot longer to pull than we'd imagined. We'd like to be open by August at the latest, but with construction, you just never know what can happen."

A line formed between her brows. "You'll have crews here all day?"

And then it hit him. She was worried about what that was going to do to her business—the soft pink, feminine business that happened just beyond those doors under crystal lights. Joel looked down the street. Her neighbors included an antique shop, florist, holistic healing, and a bakery on the end cap. Something told him he was going to be met with the same lack of sensitivity from each of them as well.

But his father always taught him to keep to his convictions.

He believed in what he was doing, and nothing was going to stop him. So, he was going to inconvenience people for a while, but he was also about to bring in three times the number of customers to the quaint little square.

Holding out his hand he began to introduce himself. "Joel Kingsley."

The woman hesitantly took his hand and shook it. Her nail polish matched the door and her lipstick.

He'd expected a weak little shake, but he got a full on business handshake, and it lit something inside him.

"Kennedy Devereaux."

"*Kennedy Devereaux Designs*, that's you."

"Of course it is."

"You have a nice place. What do you do?"

"Fashion design."

He shook his head and then looked down at his worn boots. "This is my fashion. So what does fashion design mean?"

Her lips pursed as she hiked a pink and gray leather bag up on her shoulder. "I design the accent jewelry that I sell. And then I help women put together exquisite outfits with designer clothing. One on one."

"I didn't see a lot of clothes."

"No, I keep them in the back. I help women build their wardrobe so that they don't look as if they'd walked out of a GAP."

He wanted to laugh, but the woman in front of him had a no nonsense way about her, and he found it quite intimidated and excited him all at the same time.

"I look forward to seeing your store sometime," he said. "And I'll be next door all the time, so if you need anything at all…"

"I can't imagine I will."

Ouch, he thought. "Well, if you do, you'll find me." He pulled a card from his pocket and handed it to her. "My cell number is on there too. Call anytime."

She held the card between her perfectly manicured fingers. "Tap house?"

"Yeah. Like all the breweries you see around, only we don't brew. We just serve."

"A bar?"

"Tap house. Different feel. More community," he corrected.

Kennedy shook her head and dropped his card into the void of her bag. "I hope it doesn't disturb the quaintness. Olde Town is such a lovely place."

"We intend to add to the loveliness. You'll see," he promised. Kennedy turned to the pink door he'd been looking through and unlocked it. As she pushed it open, Joel lifted a hand to wave. "It was nice to meet you."

She turned in the doorway, and he realized she belonged right there. She was as pink and feminine as the store. "You as well," she said as she shut the door and locked it from the inside.

That could have gone better, he thought as he turned and looked at the little town square that would be his home of sorts. Olde Town, as it was called, was a park in the center square with an enormous gazebo. He remembered his mother walking the park as he and his brother played on the playground when they were little. Back then, all the stores that lined the quiet and quaint streets were mostly antique stores. There was the penny candy store, which he had seen had been turned into an ice cream shop.

Most of the antique stores were gone, but the center square still held that mystique.

He turned back to see Kennedy moving about her store. She lifted her head and looked at him, and he waved again. Oh, he'd win her over. Change was hard for some people.

She'd get used to it—and him.

CHAPTER 2

*K*ennedy watched the man outside her store. Not uneasy on the eyes in his scuffed up work books and Carhartt T-shirt. But he was out of place, and shouldn't the others in the neighborhood have a say in that?

There was already a bar in Olde Town, and it was nicely situated on the other side of the square so it never had to bother her or her business. But a tap house next door, really?

She set her bag down in the office she kept in the back. It complemented the front of her store with a white desk and a fluffy pink rug, which she would often run her bare feet over just to ease any tension she might have with a persnickety client. But it was too damn early in the morning to even consider that, since she'd just walked in.

Kennedy looked at her planner spread out on her desk and color coordinated in pink and yellow. Cara and Hillary both would work since it was Monday. The store wasn't as busy, and they didn't take appointments on Mondays, but the shipments would come in and need to be cataloged, hung, and steamed. There was always the occasional foot traffic, and it never failed that she'd sell a piece or two of her jewelry.

She looked down at the bracelet she wore. She loved the beads she'd used; pearls and opaques. She'd made three of them, and she'd put them out on the display.

As she tended to her emails, she admired her freshly manicured nails. Sarah, her nail technician, had her scheduled for weekly manicures on Monday mornings. Not only did it start the week off just right to gossip and be pampered, but a fresh coat of *Kennedy Pink* was just what she needed after a weekend of building jewelry.

Kennedy walked to the small break room and started up her coffee pot. She watered the plant near the sink and looked out the window. The man she'd met out front—Joel—stood with three other men looking up at the old building, which still said post office on the side that faced Kennedy's store.

They pointed at the building, made notes, laughed, and scratched their heads. Then, as if they could all feel her looking at them, they all turned and smiled at her. Joel waved, and she waved back before quickly moving away from the window.

Construction hadn't even started and it was already distracting her.

She heard the front door unlock and the bell above it chime before the lock was reengaged.

"Kennedy, I'm here," Cara called from the front door.

"Making coffee."

She could hear her footsteps grow closer on the hardwood floor. When she turned around, coffee mug in hand, Cara stood in the doorway, glowing.

She was eight months pregnant and wore it like a badge of honor—which it was.

"I can't wait until coffee smells good again," she said as she winced.

"I'm sorry. I should make this at home and bring it with me."

Cara waved off Kennedy's comment with her hand. "If I worried about every smell that made me sick, I'd have to live in a bubble. Remember those chocolate chip muffins I used to love at the bakery? Barf fest. Can't even look at them now," she said as she signed in on the time sheet. "Carrots. All I want are carrots."

"That's good, right?"

Cara shrugged. "I'm supposed to want junk and be allowed it, right? Oh, no. Not me. I crave carrots," she laughed as she walked to the other room to begin her day.

Kennedy leaned against the counter and smiled into her mug. Children had never been on her radar. Perhaps that was because she'd been brought up to know she wasn't an important child.

She sipped her coffee and scolded herself. Okay, that was a load of crap. Her parents loved her. Her father was just a mess of a man, and that messed up what could have been her perfect story.

Then again, she had learned from years of working with women in an intimate setting, almost like therapy, that hardly anyone had a perfect childhood.

Out of curiosity, she turned back and looked out the window one more time at the group of men, which had now expanded by three more. She let out a breath.

She could look at the new business as a burden and a direct insult to her, or she could enjoy the view of the men who stood looking up at the old building.

The one she'd met was a looker, and a couple others were too. Okay, the positive would be that there would be hunky men building a business next to her. Seriously, that couldn't be bad, she thought as she moved back to her office. Not that she needed a hunky man to watch, but she was still human. She loved to look pretty, and she liked to appreciate the look of a rugged man.

CHAPTER 3

The newest bracelets were displayed on the small table nearest the front door. Kennedy had her entire store staged so that those just browsing would look at the handmade pieces, the ones that were reasonably priced, and continue to walk inside. Had she put the custom pieces by the door, most people would look and walk right back out. This she knew from experience.

She looked around her little store, the pastel tones pleasing to the eye. It was exactly what she'd dreamed of since she was a small girl. Again, she looked down at her newly polished nails, and then rearranged the signature bottles of the polish on the counter.

Sarah had helped her create the color, and they'd had it bottled. It was a favorite with the middle school crowd, but they wouldn't be thirteen forever. Someday, those same girls would come and buy jewelry, and then they'd come for the clothes that Kennedy kept in the back. And that was where the real money was made. Most of her clients spent two thousand dollars every season on new pieces. And some of those clients were the wives of the men on the city council who had thumbed their noses at her when they'd first walked through her door.

The reflection from a car parking outside her store caught her eye, and the whistle from Hillary. "Holy cow! Look at that!"

Hillary moved to the door and pulled it open.

Kennedy shook her head and followed.

A white, stretch Hummer limousine was parked at the curb. New plates, and that hit Kennedy right in the chest.

The driver skirted the front and removed his glasses as Hillary moved to him. "Let me see inside. Oh, this one is a gem," she said.

Kennedy watched as her brother, Chase, gave Hillary a grin and then opened the door for her.

Like a small child, Hillary climbed inside.

"This is new," Kennedy said, and she noted her own displeased tone.

"Already booked, too. Three weddings, a prom, and a bachelorette party," he informed her with a raise of his brows.

"This is what you borrowed the money for? I thought you were upgrading the other one. Actually, I thought you were going to put it toward your house."

Chase wrapped his arm around Kennedy's shoulders. "Think big, sis. This is three. I almost have a fleet."

"A fleet of debt."

"Not for long. The other two are almost paid off."

"And employment costs? Insurance? Chase…"

"You're not the only business-minded Devereaux around. Yes, I borrowed the money for this and not the house. I could live in this if I have to. You'll get your money back."

She had no doubt, but she'd have rather thought her money was going to a home for her brother. Then again, a two bedroom in the suburbs wasn't his style. A big car full of drunk girls, that was more his pace.

Kennedy heard the whistles long before she saw the men walk around the side of the building.

"Nice ride," one of the men said.

"Is this to pick up a customer?" Joel asked as he rounded the corner.

Kennedy pushed her shoulders back, urging Chase to drop his arm. "My brother runs a limo service. This is his new acquisition."

"Nice." Joel held out his hand. "Joel Kingsley."

"Chase Devereaux," her brother said as he shook his hand.

"This is my brother, Jeff, and our business partners Oliver and Craig," Joel introduced the other men to Chase, and then they shook her hand as well. "We're turning the old post office into a tap room. Just getting started on the renovations."

Chase's eyes went wide. "Tap room? Damn, that's just what we need around here. The antique stores and candy shops are old school."

Kennedy nudged her brother with her elbow, and he shrugged her off.

"Mind showing me your plans?" Chase asked and a moment later followed the men back to the old building.

Kennedy watched them disappear as Hillary climbed from the limo. "You should go sit in there, Ken," she offered, not seeing Kennedy wince at the shortening of her name that her family and friends sometimes used. "There is enough room for twenty people in there, and you could dance in the middle. I have got to have a party just so I can get driven around in this thing."

Pressing her fingertips to her temples, Kennedy watched as Hillary climbed back into the limo again, and this time she called for Cara to join her.

Joel walked around the back of the building with Chase in tow. "Limo business, huh?" he asked and Chase moved next to him.

"Yeah. Started it as a hobby, and then full time when I got downsized in the field I was in."

"What was that?"

"Financial. All the better. I can rock a suit just fine, but being stuck in a building all day, that's just not my style. I had a lead on a few cars, took out a loan, and started business. When you have to make it to pay the bills, you make it."

Joel laughed. That was his philosophy too. "I'd like to see this up and running, too. I don't like having those loans accumulating interest and no income."

"When is your target date to open?"

"Ideally we'd like to hit mid-August. Timing didn't work out to get into the building sooner."

"City hold you back?"

Joel shrugged. "It took a bit, but this is exactly the kind of business that goes into places like this. Every city is changing the look of their older areas, and tap houses and restaurants are just what they need."

"So you'll have a kitchen too?"

Joel shook his head and smiled. "Food trucks."

"I like it. I'm sure Kennedy thumbed her nose at you, though."

The expression she'd worn when she'd looked at his business card had entered his mind. "She didn't look too happy. She called us a bar."

"Ouch."

"Yeah. I think once we're up and running, she'll see it won't be so bad. This is the second tap room we've done. We sold the other a little over a year ago, and then this fell into our lap. It seemed like the right thing to do."

Chase nodded. "She'll get over it. She likes things pretty and pink. This will be far from that."

The comment caused Joel to laugh. He could have pegged her for that type of girl from the front door of her shop, even before he'd laid eyes on her. And when he saw her for the first time, well, that was something he knew he'd never forget.

"C'mon, let me show you around. Maybe you can talk your sister into thinking I'm not such a bad guy."

CHAPTER 4

*I*t was nearly an hour before Chase popped his head into the store and said goodbye to Kennedy, and then moved that monstrosity from the street. Because she had a dark side, she looked up the value of the limousine he'd driven up in. Yeah, she thought as she looked at the number on the screen, she'd never see that money again. There was no way in hell he'd be able to pay her back just driving it around. The gas alone was going to keep him in the poor house. But, as Chase had said, he could live in it.

When Kennedy walked into the break room for her afternoon cup of coffee, Cara was seated at the small table, her feet propped up on the adjacent chair.

"Do you want to sit? I'll move."

Kennedy shook her head. "No need. You take a minute. Are your ankles doing okay?"

"Sure. It's my back today. I'm not going to complain though. I wanted this baby so bad, that I'll take every ache and pain along with it."

Kennedy smiled as she poured her coffee and thought of the

years and money that had been invested in that baby Cara spoke of. Yes, little Melody McEwan would be loved and doted on.

The very thought brought tears to Kennedy's eyes, and she turned toward the window to compose herself. Kennedy had always been the kind of woman to go after anything she wanted, and she'd get it. Even as a child, she could do her fair share of manipulating her mother and father into what she wanted, but then again, the fact that she was tossed around between them was their fault. She used that to her advantage. But she'd never wanted something like a baby, not in the way Cara had. She and her husband had gone through years of infertility and treatments, only to nearly lose hope and a lot of money.

But then it happened.

Kennedy immediately had told Cara to stay home, but she'd refused. Nothing needed to change until the baby arrived, she'd assured her. Besides, she'd been so focused on getting pregnant, she didn't want to spend the whole pregnancy alone at home worrying about it. Being at the store was the best for Cara, and Kennedy loved having her around.

As she sipped her coffee, she noticed that Joel was seated on the tailgate of his truck eating from a paper bag. Didn't he look cute with his feet dangling as he lifted a homemade sandwich to his lips?

Perhaps she'd take her coffee out back and make nice. She felt as if she hadn't made the nicest impression when she'd met him that morning.

"You've been busy today," she said from the back door of her shop, and Joel's head lifted.

"This will be the norm for a while. Sixteen-hour days."

Kennedy walked toward his truck. "My brother was impressed with your plans."

"He said it would be his kind of place."

The thought that it was just a fancy bar crossed Kennedy's

mind, but she'd refrain from inserting her opinions. "He'll be a good customer."

Joel took another bite of his sandwich. "You don't have anyone shopping in the back of your store?" he asked with a smile.

"Not on Mondays. Restock, and walk-ins only."

"Got it." He finished his sandwich. "Want a walk through?"

Kennedy gripped her mug between her hands tighter. "Have you started working on it?"

"Not much. But I can point out what we're doing."

She looked back at her store, noticing that both Cara and Hillary were watching her from the window in the break room. She should go back to work, or her employees would be standing there until she returned. However, she did want to see what was going to go on next door. There was no stopping the business going in. If she was supportive, perhaps it wouldn't reflect badly on her own business, but still, it was just a bar.

"I have a few minutes."

Joel hopped off the tailgate and crumpled up his empty lunch bag. The guys had gone for Mexican food, but he preferred to watch what went into his body.

Kennedy walked toward his truck, taking steps carefully on the gravel, and he noticed she was in heels. How the hell women worked in shoes like that was beyond him, but he supposed that was part of the business woman who worked behind the pink doors. Who was she outside the pink doors he wondered?

He opened the back door to the cab of his truck and pulled out two hard hats, handing Kennedy one.

She examined it before reaching for it with her delicate fingers. "Why do I need this if you haven't started yet?"

"We have started. Just enough that I don't want any accidents. Would you like to borrow some work boots?"

Pouring her coffee cup out into the dirt, she put the hat on. "I'll be just fine."

And he was sure she would be.

Joel found that he wanted to take her arm and guide her through the back door, but something told him she wasn't the kind of woman who would appreciate it.

He led the way, staying close enough just in case she might need his stability.

"We're working on getting the dividing walls down. That should be done by the end of the week. They had it broken into three different retail spaces."

"I've been next door for years. I know what it looked like."

"Right," he said realizing she'd probably been in the building many times. "Then you know it's been empty for nearly a year. Without occupants, a building can go downhill fast."

"So there are problems?"

"Not really, but it needs work. We'll add the necessary supports, take down the walls, and start refurbishing everything." They stepped into the semi-open space and stopped again. "There are the post office boxes we uncovered." He pointed to the exposed wall.

Kennedy took a few steps in. "Are you going to keep them there?"

"I think so. It will tie in the neighborhood vibe. The bar will go over here," he motioned with his hand. "Tables in the middle, and out front we will make patio seating. We'll replace the front windows with rolling doors, so we can open up the entire inside when it's nice, and close it off when it's cold."

She turned toward him and her blue eyes narrowed on him. "Will you serve food?"

He thought about the conversation he'd had with her brother, and he wondered if telling her about the food trucks was a good idea. There were no other choices. She'd know about them sooner or later.

"We'll have food truck service off the side street."

He saw her lips purse, and she took a moment. "So they won't be out front?"

"No."

Kennedy nodded slowly, and he figured that was the best he could have hoped for.

"Well, it looks like you have your work cut out for you."

"This is the fun part."

"Thank you for the tour," she said as she headed back to the door and stepped outside before pulling the hard hat off and handing it back to him. "Best of luck."

Joel took the hat and watched as Kennedy walked back to her store gracefully, disappearing through the back door, and the two faces in the window that had been watching them disappeared too.

CHAPTER 5

*J*oel stepped out of his truck just shy of six o'clock in the morning. His drive in had offered him a beautiful sunrise, and he figured that was payment for his early start. The past two weeks had produced a lot of progress on the tap room. So far they were right on track, but that made him nervous. If they were going to run into problems, he'd like to run into them at the start of the project, and not at the end when it would be more costly. Then again, when did things ever work out like that?

He grabbed his coffee mug and pulled out his hard hat, placing it on his head before taking a walk to the front of the building.

As if it were habit now, he looked at the pink entrance to the boutique next door. He hadn't seen Kennedy much in the two weeks that they'd been working on the building. He'd catch a glimpse of her coming or going, and she'd give him a friendly wave, but there had been no more conversation between them, which had been disappointing.

There were new planters flanking the entry—pastel just like the inside of the store. He'd never known anyone so elegant and the thought drew him right to his mother, which was funny. She'd had a career before she had kids, so he'd seen the power suits and clothes in her closet, that only made their appearance for formal events. When she'd become a mother, she was fully engaged in jeans and tennis shoes. When he and his brother had grown up and moved away, his parents became world travelers, and those suits were boxed up and given away.

Joel assumed, though, his mother had the same kind of passion for work as Kennedy did.

For the past few weeks he'd watched women come and go from the store, sometimes helped to their cars with garment bags on hangers and other bags with handles. The amount of money in and out of that store had to be quite a bit, he thought. But who would look at that store and think that? No one, and wasn't that part of its charm?

He'd mention the store to his mother. She would enjoy it, and he'd like to get her take on Kennedy Devereaux.

Joel walked to the front of his building as his brother turned the corner, hard hat on and coffee in hand. "Going too smoothly," he said as he lifted his mug to his lips.

Joel nodded. "I was thinking that too. Maybe the building wanted to be used for this project, so it's happy."

Jeff snorted a laugh. "Now you're a building whisperer?"

With a shrug, Joel moved to the door, which was covered in paper from the inside. He rested his ear to it and nodded. "Yep, she's a happy building."

Shaking his head, Jeff blew out a breath. "You're a nut. Sampling today at noon," he reminded him as he started back around the side of the building.

"That's my favorite day of these projects," Joel admitted as he followed his brother. "I was going to call Mom and tell her she should check out the boutique next door."

Jeff turned and looked at the building. "It's a girlie place. She might like it."

"The women that come and go make me think of Mom's career years."

"We weren't around for those."

"I know, but the pictures of her in her heels and suits."

"And that big hair?" Jeff mused.

"Yeah. Maybe she'd like something nice. I could buy her a gift certificate or something."

Jeff opened the back of his truck and pulled out his tool belt. "You should do that. Then again you could just go talk to the woman."

"What woman?"

"Kennedy," he said as he strapped on the belt. "I'm not an idiot. I see you looking over there every time the damn door opens, trying to get a glimpse of her."

Joel shook his head as he, too, opened the back of his truck for his tools. "She seemed nice enough when she came over and walked through."

"She seemed put off as if we were going to drive her business away. See, you're smitten, because we all see a bitch factor and all you see is the pink."

Joel pulled a bucket from the back of his truck and set it on the ground. "When was she ever bitchy? Seriously, you all think that's how she is?"

"She's got her agenda, and we have ours. No, she wasn't bitchy. I'm sorry I hurt your feelings. She did, however, come across like that girl in *Legally Blonde*. I just didn't see her dog in her purse." Jeff laughed as he disappeared inside and Joel stood a moment longer to look up at the window he knew went to Kennedy's break room.

She'd been out of her element the day he'd dragged her through the construction, but he hadn't thought she seemed bitchy. Was he smitten?

He laughed off the thought as he closed the back of his truck and locked it. Picking up the bucket, he looked at the window again wondering if he'd see her peering out of it later.

Yeah, he was going to buy his mother a gift certificate. Not only would he finally get to see inside the store, he could have some more face time with Kennedy too. Maybe he'd see what the others saw—but he hoped not.

CHAPTER 6

*K*ennedy admired her fresh manicure as she lounged in her office. Sometimes Mondays felt like cheating on her business; a manicure first thing in the morning, and no scheduled clients to dress. She was still at work, she thought as she looked at the emails sitting on her computer screen awaiting answers, but as she ran her bare feet over the soft rug under her desk, she felt the ease of not having to attend to them in timely manner.

Deciding on another cup of coffee, Kennedy walked to the break room and watched the progress on the tap house next door. There were more trucks there than last week, and hadn't Gladys, the florist, mentioned there was already more traffic on the street when she'd delivered the bouquets for the showroom? Progress, Kennedy had decided, was inevitable. As long as she didn't have drunks wandering into her store during the day, and no one broke in at night, she'd find peace with having a bar next door.

As she waited for the pot to finish brewing, she spotted Joel walking out of the building and immediately looking her way. Did he know she was standing there? He waved, and she waved back. Then he held up a finger as if to keep her in place as he hurried toward the back door.

Panic zipped through Kennedy, realizing she didn't even have her shoes on. Hurrying to her office, she pulled her heels out from under her desk, and hobbled back to the break room pulling them on as Joel opened the back door.

"Did I catch you at a bad time?" He looked at her from the doorway as she nearly fell into the counter trying to balance on one leg and pull on her other shoe.

"No. We're good here. What can I do for you?"

Joel stepped into the break room and quickly looked around, before focusing his attention back on Kennedy.

"I wanted to buy a gift certificate for my mom for your store."

"Last minute Mother's Day shopping?"

His eyes went wide. "Oh, hell. That is this week, isn't it?"

"Sunday."

"Yeah. Well, it was just going to be a nice gesture, but now I guess it'll be a Mother's Day gift. Thanks for saving my ass."

Kennedy let out a soft laugh. "Trust me, I will see my share of frantic men in here this week doing the same thing. I'm prepared. C'mon," she said, nodding to the doorway.

Joel followed her to the front of the store, and they were both met with odd looks from Hillary and Cara.

"I don't know if you've met my co-workers, Hillary and Cara."

Both women held up hands in waves as they unpacked boxes.

Joel lifted his hand, returning the gesture. "I'm Joel Kingsley. One of the owners of the tap house next door." Both women smiled, and he turned toward Kennedy standing behind the counter. "It's nice in here."

"I work very hard to make it that way."

"Fresh flowers. Pastel colors." He picked up one of the bottles of nail polish that was displayed on the counter. "*Kennedy Pink*? You designed your own nail polish too?"

Kennedy splayed her hand on the counter to acknowledge the

custom shade of pink. "It's big with the middle school crowd," she said, and he laughed as he replaced the bottle.

"I will guarantee my mother will buy a bottle of that. I've never known her to turn her back on a trendy color of nail polish."

"I look forward to meeting her," Kennedy admitted as she opened the drawer that housed the elegant gift certificates, pink with gold foil overlay. "What is your mother's name?"

Joel looked up at her, his eyes searching as if he'd forgotten his mother's name. "Oh, sorry, June?"

A smile tugged at the corners of Kennedy's mouth. "Are you sure?"

"Yeah," he chuckled. "I'm sure. June Kingsley."

Kennedy began to write his mother's name on the gift certificate and Joel leaned in over the counter.

"Holy shit," he said and then backed up and whispered it again, "holy shit. You can whip out a pen and write in calligraphy?"

Kennedy lifted her eyes to meet his. "Yes."

"That's the coolest thing ever. My mother is going to fall in love with you."

The smile that had only tugged at her lips now fully formed. "You're a businessman. Isn't that the goal? The first rule in building a clientele is to make them fall in love with you? It's the little touches," she said as she finished the name of the certificate. "How much would you like to put on it?"

Joel shrugged and leaned in again. "How much do people spend here?"

Kennedy capped the pen she was using. "Well, I have walk in traffic that buys a few custom pieces of my costume jewelry and a bottle of polish, of course."

"Of course."

"Then a few purchase purses or the few clothing items I have on display."

"My mother never met a purse she didn't like."

"I love her already," Kennedy teased. "Then, there is the exclusive shopping appointments that I do."

"The secret stash of nice stuff hidden in the back."

"Right," she laughed. "If you're just getting her in the front door, fifty to one hundred would be nice. If you want to spoil her rotten, minimum five hundred."

Kennedy was sure he'd started to sweat when she said that. "Five hundred?"

"My least expensive clothing in the back goes for two hundred, and most women don't leave with only one outfit."

Joel leaned his forearms on the top of the counter and studied her. His dark eyes pulled at her, and she took a purposeful step back to pull the stool toward her to sit before her knees gave out.

"The minute I met you I thought of my mother."

Well, she thought, that was the least sexy thing he could have said as he looked at her like that.

"Thank you?"

Joel chuckled. "I mean before my brother and I were born, my mom was a successful business woman. That late seventies, early eighties corporate ladder-climbing woman. Business suits, heels, big hair."

"Modern woman taking over the world."

"Yes," he said with admiration. "By the time I came along, she'd given up that life to be a mother. And she was—is—a damn good one, and she could rock a pair of jeans and sneakers. She's always had her hair done and her makeup on, even if we were just playing in the house for the day. There was always a schedule on the fridge under a magnet that laid out the day."

Kennedy's eyes shifted to the agenda she had, color coded, next to the register. "She sounds like just the woman who shops here."

Joel pulled his wallet from his back pocket and handed her five crisp one hundred dollar bills. She wondered why he'd seemed so surprised by the figure when he obviously had no problem producing that kind of money for a purchase.

"She deserves something awesome," he said as he put his wallet back in his pocket.

"Most mothers do." She continued writing out the gift certificate. "Your parents are still married?"

"Forty-five years," he threw out the number without having to consider it. "They're kinda gross about it too. Still kiss in public and say gooey things to each other."

Kennedy couldn't help but laugh loud enough that the girls turned to look at her. Acknowledging that, she focused on sliding the gift certificate into the envelope. "I think that's very sweet."

"Your parents?"

"Not married. In fact, it's a long twisted story."

"I'd love to hear it," Joel offered and Kennedy felt the blood drain from her head.

"My parents' story?"

"Yeah, maybe we could have dinner."

"You and me?"

Joel nodded slowly. "If dinner is too much, maybe we could walk to the other side of the square one afternoon and have ice cream."

"Ice cream," she repeated, now not sure how she should act around him.

"I'll tell you what. After you're done here today, come by the tap room. We're doing a tasting at noon and I'll have some growlers left over. I'd love your opinion on the selection we're considering."

"Beer?"

"Yes," he chuckled again. "You leave the store at six?"

Now she narrowed her eyes on him. "How do you know that?"

"We're neighbors. If it's any consolation, Gladys gets to work at ten and leaves by four. I'd say that's no way to run a business, but I see the delivery truck pull up to her back door and load up on funeral arrangements every day. She has a good business, and I assume the front door stuff is just for extra cash."

"You've watched her that much?"

"Part of becoming a new member of a community that's already tight-knit, you have to be observant and know what's happening around you. I know that you drink your coffee over the sink in your break room and watch us."

That horrified her, but before she could counter with anything, that would have probably been gibberish anyway, he held up a hand.

"It's the norm," he said. "I'd be disappointed if no one was paying attention. So, come over around six?"

Kennedy noticed her two employees looking her way and nodding. What was she supposed to do now?

"I will come over at six. But not for long. I do have other things to do."

"Of course you do. I'll see you then."

He held out his hand, and she handed him the gift certificate.

"She's going to love this. Thank you." Joel turned to acknowledge Cara and Hillary. "It was nice to meet you both."

Then, he let himself out the front door, pulling it closed behind him.

CHAPTER 7

*K*ennedy busied herself at the register, entering the gift certificate details into the computer, putting the cash in the drawer, and avoiding eye contact with the two women who had stopped working and waited for her attention.

"What?" she finally blurted out as she nearly slammed the cash drawer closed.

Hillary helped Cara to her feet, and they both hurried across the store.

Hillary propped her elbows up on the counter. "You're having drinks with him?"

"I'm going over to taste whatever they're bringing in."

"They're bringing in beer. It's a tap house."

Cara shook her head and rested her hands on her stomach. "You agreed to have a beer with the guy. The guy you try to catch a peek of every time you get coffee."

Hillary looked at Cara. "Have you noticed her coffee consumption has gone up in the past two weeks?"

"I have."

Both women turned their eyes back to Kennedy who had resigned herself to sitting on the stool and laughing.

"He's handsome," Kennedy admitted.

"He's freaking hot," Hillary said, turning back toward the box she and Cara had been emptying. "He's hot. His brother's hot. Those partners of his are hot. The guy who came to check the building yesterday, was hot."

That caused Kennedy and Cara to both laugh.

Kennedy hopped off the stool, carried it to the other side of the counter, and motioned to Cara to hop on as she helped Hillary with the box.

"I'm not looking for love."

"Who said anything about love?" Hillary asked as she pulled a new leather purse from the box. "You haven't dated in years. Years," she reminded her. "So have a thing with the good-looking bar keep."

Kennedy sat back on her heels. "I would never have a thing, and you know it."

"Yeah, yeah." Hillary displayed the purse on the shelf. "You'll never have a thing or any fun because your dad had a thing. You're not your dad."

"My dad ruined his family with that thing," she reminded them. "Anyway, it's just a beer."

Cara hopped off the stool and walked toward them, touching one of the pendants Kennedy had designed on her way across the shop. "You deserve a little something on the romantic side, and he's not your type, so maybe this will be fun."

"I have a type?"

Both women nodded.

Hillary sat back on her heels. "Business suit and tie. Nice car. Bottle of wine and flowers. Condo downtown."

The churning in Kennedy's stomach didn't help her nerves. She did have a type, and there she sat on the floor of her store, assuming she didn't need a little thing with someone. Were they saying she was dull and unhappy, because she was happy. She had her business and her little house a few miles away. Just that morning she had rosebuds on her rose bush, and a few tulips popping their heads out of the soil in her garden. That made her happy.

"I guess I know what I like," she defended herself as she stood.

"If you knew what you liked, you'd be happy when you found it," Hillary said pulling out another purse from the box.

Kennedy shook her head and headed back to her desk when she realized she'd forgotten about the cup of coffee she'd gone into the break room for in the first place.

She headed for the coffee maker, and out of habit, she looked out the window to see Joel looking down at plans with another man on the tailgate of his truck.

He wasn't her type at all, she thought looking at the dirty jeans and worn boots. The pickup had a dent in the tailgate, and it amused her that he hadn't fixed it. Then, as if he felt her looking at him, he raised his head and turned her way, giving her a smile and a nod in her direction in lieu of a wave.

Not wanting to appear rude, she lifted her mug in salute, also an acknowledgment that she had other reasons to be standing there, and not just to look at him.

AT NOON, Joel sat down with his brother at a makeshift table while they waited for the others. Because Jeff was the kind of guy to think of everything, he had a foot-long sandwich cut into small slices, a box of crackers, and a peanut bar mix from Costco on the table.

"Lunch and a sampling?" Joel mused as he pulled back a folding chair and sat down.

"Can't have you all drunk in the middle of the day, now can I? Then what will that pretty woman in the pink think of us?"

"Funny."

"I saw you go over there. Through the back door. Now that was intimate."

Joel leaned in, resting his elbows on the table. "It's even more pink in the store. Mom is going to love it."

"You got her a gift certificate?"

"I did. Five freaking hundred."

Jeff opened the bar mix and scooped out a handful. "You spent five hundred dollars in her store?"

"She even has custom nail polish."

Jeff laughed as she poured the handful of mix into his mouth. "Mom does like a nice nail polish."

"She's coming over here at six to have a drink with me. I told her I'd like her opinion on what we sample."

"Who? Mom?"

"Kennedy, you moron." Joel pulled the bar mix toward him and took a handful.

"And she drinks beer?"

Joel took a peanut from the mix in his hand and popped it into his mouth. "I can't imagine it's her drink of choice, but she said she'd be here."

"Do you think it's wise to date the woman with the business next door? If she hates you, it could be bad for us."

The thought hadn't really crossed his mind. He was too immersed in the scent of her and the pink of her. "It'll be fine. I don't think she likes me as it is."

Jeff shook his head. "And that's why you see her in the window all the time? She's not looking at you?"

Joel popped another peanut into his mouth. "Maybe she's smitten with Oliver," he said as the man walked into the room with their other partner Craig and boxes of growlers and cans.

"Who's smitten with me?" Oliver asked as he set his box on the table. "Oh, tell me it's that gal next door."

Joel discarded the rest of the bar mix in his hand into the bucket they'd placed for trash under the table. Oliver's words had felt like a kick in the gut, and Jeff must have noticed. Without hesitation, he kicked again.

"Which gal next door?" his brother asked. "The blonde in the pink and heels?"

Ouch, Joel thought as Oliver took a seat.

"Are you kidding me? Too pretentious. Too stuck up. I've been snubbed by the cheerleading squad and the prom queen before." He began to unload the box he'd set on the table. "I'm talking the other one. Not the pregnant one either," he said holding up a finger in objection before one of the mentioned her. "The leggy one with the mess of auburn hair. Sexy as hell. Like maybe, she was the wannabe jock that fit in with the pretty girls and balanced them out. You know."

They all howled in laughter at his analogy, except for Joel who was able to finally breathe. Good, he thought. No one had their sights set on Kennedy except him. But Jeff was right. If she ended up hating him, it could be bad for them.

As Oliver cracked open the first growler and passed around the plastic cups, Joel decided he couldn't afford for Kennedy to hate him.

They all lifted their cups in the air to salute to the tap house. He lifted his in honor of Kennedy—the woman who would fall madly in love with him and never want to hate him. He'd make sure of that.

CHAPTER 8

*T*he bell over the front door chimed for the last time as Hillary walked out of store and locked the door behind her.

Kennedy eased back in her desk chair, her bare feet making circles on her plush rug. It was six o'clock, and she had to decide if she was really going to go next door and drink a beer with Joel, or she was going to forget all about it and go home.

Turning off her computer, she sat in silence for a moment longer.

Oh, to hell with it, she thought. He intrigued her. She absolutely was going next door to have a beer, even if that sounded like a horrible idea.

Kennedy turned off the lights in the shop, made sure the coffee pot was off as well, and left through the back door, locking it. When she turned toward the tap house, she noticed Joel standing at the back door, his body leaned casually up against the door jamb. Her heart rate quickened. Those dirty jeans and worn out work boots had a sexy appeal, and she had to suck in the air that was now thick around her.

It was a beer, she reminded herself. Just a drink with the guy next door.

"I came out to make sure you were still over there. I thought you'd blown me off," he said as she started toward him.

Pulling her purse up onto her shoulder, she felt the tug of guilt at his statement. She'd considered blowing him off, but she wouldn't tell him that.

"I said I was coming, didn't I? Well, here I am." She didn't much care for her tone. It made her sound conceited. She was used to that depiction and probably deserved it.

"Here you are."

The light from inside glowed at his back, as the shadows from outside made his eyes darken. Kennedy gripped her purse strap to gain some control. He was handsome and just a little mysterious—and completely not her type.

"Are you going to invite me in?" she asked, and he nodded slowly.

"We tasted thirty beers. I'm moving just a bit slow." A smile crept over his mouth, and she found hers went dry.

"We can do this another day."

"Nah, I have a couple I want your opinion on." He reached a hand out to her as if they were casual enough friends, and she would take it—and she did.

Joel led her into the tap room, which now looked more bare than it had two weeks earlier. The walls were bare, only studs and wires. The wall of old mail boxes was covered with a tarp, but there was, what she assumed would be, a bar.

In the center of the room was a makeshift table made from two barrels and a slat of wood. Around it were four folding chairs. The walls that had once divided the building into individual locations were now gone.

"So this is your place? I like what you've done with it," she joked and it warranted a laugh from Joel who still held her hand and led her to the table.

"We open tomorrow. Critics say that people don't like to hold their drinks all night, but I think we have something original happening here."

Now she laughed. He was easy to be around, and she wondered when she could let down her guard.

"Table for two," he offered as he let go of her hand and pulled out a chair for her.

"Thank you."

Kennedy sat down and looked around as Joel took the seat next to her. "Did your partners all drive home then?"

Joel nodded, then shook his head. "Well, Oliver and Craig drove home. But they didn't do as much tasting as Jeff and I did. So Jeff's wife picked him up."

"No one offered to take you home?" The moment the words were out of her mouth she wanted to retract them.

Joel smiled at her. "It's early yet," he played right into her statement.

Fisting her hands under the table, she convinced herself not to continue the conversation on that path. She was there for a drink, and that was all.

"Okay," Joel began as he set a row of plastic cups in front of her and a bowl of something that looked like dog treats. "There are five of these that I want your opinion on."

"Five? I can't drink five beers."

He smiled. "I don't want you to drink five beers," his words slurred slightly. "I want you to taste them. You can spit it out if you want."

"I'm not going to spit drinks out in front of you."

"Just sip." He opened one of the growlers and poured just enough in the cup to give her a taste. "This one is a chocolate and coffee infused beer. Jeff's wife likes it the best, so there is less of it, because she had a glass too."

Kennedy tried not to laugh. She had to wonder just how many beers he had before she got there. But it was part of the process, just as her flying to Paris and New York twice a year was part of her process.

As she picked up the cup and lifted it to her lips she watched him watching her. "Are you having any?"

He smiled again. "Are you driving me home?"

"Well, right now I don't think you should drive yourself, but I didn't anticipate driving you home."

"Try it. We will discuss me getting home when we're done."

Kennedy lifted the cup to her mouth, but held it just beneath her nose. Was she supposed to smell it? Swirl it in the cup? Slowly, she took a sip and then licked her lips. That wasn't half bad, she decided.

"I like that." She finished the small taste in her cup. "Oh, I think this one is a must. I didn't know chocolate and coffee could be mixed in a beer."

"I thought you'd like that one." He opened another growler and poured its contents into another cup. "This one is citrus. More specifically, grapefruit."

"Seriously?"

"Seriously."

She looked at the drink he'd poured for her. This one was lighter in color, more like a beer should look, she thought. She repeated the process and lifted it to her lips to smell it. Then she drank down the liquid without the same caution she'd given to the other. The moment it hit her tongue she'd wished she'd asked him where she could spit it out. The bitterness burned her throat as she swallowed it, and she let out a breath and a whimper as she put the cup down.

"Oh, that's horrible. Citrus beer should sound good, but..."

He laughed. Had he done that on purpose? "I don't like that one either, but the other three drank most of it. They love the tart beers."

"So you already decided to carry that one, and didn't really need my opinion?"

"No, I wanted your opinion. I need someone on my side."

Surely her opinion wasn't going to carry any weight.

Joel poured from another growler. "I want to see if you can decipher this one."

"I don't think I'm cut out for this job. Besides, I've had two drinks and I can feel this."

"Craft beers have more alcohol."

Kennedy narrowed her eyes on him. "So I'm going to get drunk one sip at a time?"

"Only if you're a lightweight."

Well, did it look like she was someone who could hold her own in a drinking contest? No.

"Maybe I'm not the best person do give you my opinion."

"You're the perfect person. You represent the people who live around here and do business. I want to make sure we have a selection that will speak to you, too."

"I won't order that grapefruit stuff."

"Me either," he laughed. "Food helps though."

Kennedy lifted the glass to her lips and studied him over it. "Food helps? What does that mean?"

"It absorbs the alcohol."

"So you'll serve food."

"Yes. No. What I meant was maybe we can go get something to eat to offset the alcohol."

Without tasting the liquid in the cup she set it down. "Are you asking me to dinner?"

"If it makes you feel any better, I need to eat. I would love your company. I've been dying to try that Mexican restaurant around the corner."

"It's excellent," she offered.

"What do you say? Take a walk with me? Have dinner with me —my treat. I think you still owe me the story of your parents."

They had discussed that, hadn't they?

Kennedy looked at her watch. She did need to eat. She was

intrigued by the man whose cheeks were red above the shadow of a beard.

"Okay. I'll go with you. How many more of these do you want me to taste?"

"Three more. Just sips."

"Are they as bad as that last one?"

Joel laughed as he opened the next growler. "I guess you'll have to tell me."

"Pour the drink so we can go eat," she said realizing that him sitting across from her grinning was becoming much too appealing.

However, she wasn't going to give him a ride home. That would be a mistake.

CHAPTER 9

The rest of the tasting Joel asked Kennedy to do had gone better than that second beer—the one he didn't like either, but she was sold on the rest of them. That didn't matter, they were going to carry fifty craft brewed beers from within the state, and that wasn't even half the breweries being represented.

They'd gone through the same process when they'd opened the last tap house, and Joel assumed when they sold this one, they'd do it again with the next one they opened.

Joel had locked the door when they finished, and side by side, he and Kennedy walked toward the Mexican restaurant, the sun setting at their backs and the small lights that were strung through the trees beginning to turn on.

"How far do you live from here?" he asked as the pace of their walk slowed to a stroll.

"About five miles."

"East or West?"

She shot him a short glance. "Why?"

"Curious."

"West."

"Lived here your entire life?"

She took a moment before answering, adjusting her purse on her shoulder. "On and off."

Ah, this would lead to that parental conversation he'd told her she owed him, he thought. He let the questions settle, and in silence they walked the last block to the restaurant.

Joel pulled open the door and Kennedy passed by him, as well as another couple he hadn't even seen walk up on him. When he caught up to Kennedy, she was talking to the hostess, and they were being led to the patio that overlooked the small creek that ran through the center of the town.

Kennedy had already pulled out her chair and began to sit before he could have done the gentlemanly thing of holding her chair. Well, it wasn't a date, he remembered. This was friendly conversation that he'd convinced her she owed him. If he could convince her to go on a date sometime, he'd hold that chair then.

"You've been here, what's good?" he asked as he lifted his menu and tried to adjust its distance from his eyes in the glow of twinkling lights and cloud of too many beers.

"The chimichanga is fantastic, so is the fajita. I'm partial to the grande burrito as well."

Joel laughed. "You've been here a lot."

"I've had my business for eight years. You get to know the restaurants and businesses that surround you."

That was true, and they were proof of that. Weren't they getting to know each other?

Joel looked over the menu. "I guess I had my share of carbs today. Maybe I'd better just go with the fajita straight off the plate—no tortillas." She was eyeing him, and he rested his arms on the table to look at her. "Sounds like a girl?"

"I wouldn't have said that out loud," she admitted. "But yes, I've never heard a man worry about carbs."

"More of them should. So much of our food is toxic. Seriously, do you remember kids growing up being allergic to everything? Peanuts? Milk? Food coloring?"

Kennedy opened her menu and scanned the items. "No, not really. But now I'm worried about what I'm going to eat."

Joel chuckled. "Sorry, I get a little stupid about it. Not like a lot of other people. I just like to know I can say the ingredients of the things I eat."

Kennedy closed her menu and let out a breath. "That's a good rule to live by."

The waiter arrived with two glasses of water and then folded his hands behind him to take their order by memory. Joel was never sure of that method, but usually they were spot on.

Kennedy picked up her menu. "I'll have a chicken fajita, no tortillas." She smiled at Joel as she said it, and he couldn't help but smile back.

"I'll do the same."

When the waiter walked away with the menus they handed him, Kennedy sipped her water. "You've given me something to think about."

"If I've ruined anything for you, remember you chose to adopt the philosophy yourself."

She laughed at that, and he thought for the first time since he'd met her two weeks ago, her shoulders relaxed. When she pushed her hair back, he was sure of it.

Maybe he'd ease her into that conversation about her parents now.

"So your brother owns a limo?" he asked and watched as she bit down on the straw in her water glass as she sipped.

Kennedy didn't answer right away. She finished taking her sip of water, setting in on the table, and adjusting it to her right. Then, she took a long and thoughtful breath. "Yes. He owns three of them now, I guess. This last one I lent him the money for, I assume. I thought I was giving him a down payment on a house, but..." she stopped, picked up her glass, and sipped again. "I have to remember he has a savvy business sense too, and I need to give him credit."

"You're not fond of the limo business?"

"Frivolous. That's what I think. People don't use limos every single day. Not big Hummer ones. Now his smaller car, the black one that's just pretty, he does a lot of business people back and forth to the airport. They're more comfortable to be transported by a car that doesn't say Uber or Lyft on it."

Joel nodded. "I completely understand that."

"So he has some regulars, I guess." He wondered if she was just coming to this understanding as they spoke.

"He said he's already gotten bookings for that new monstrosity. And on many occasions, our brother Max drives for him."

"New thread," Joel said as he leaned in, his elbows on the table. "You have another brother."

Kennedy picked up the glass of water again and sipped. "You're fishing for that parent story."

"You promised it to me. The full background to the living in town, on and off." He smiled at her, and she returned the gesture with a giggle. He'd gotten to her, and now he'd get the story of what made up Kennedy Devereaux.

CHAPTER 10

*S*he owed him nothing, Kennedy thought as she fixed her straw, after having bitten it closed, then took a sip of her water. The beer she'd had at his tap house was long gone now. Any courage she needed would have to be self-supplied.

Kennedy eased back in her seat and crossed her legs. With her hands on her knees, she focused on the *Kennedy Pink* polish.

"I'm the oldest of four. Well, of all of my father's children. And obviously my mother's too." Okay, maybe that wasn't obvious, and maybe it didn't have to be said. But it was how she'd started.

Kennedy adjusted in her seat and moved her water glass again before she continued. "My parents were married about three years before I was born. But that was long enough for my dad to have grown tired, and he was having an affair when my mom got pregnant. He didn't get out fast enough." Relaxing with a deep breath, Kennedy released the tension in her jaw. "The thing was, Judy, the woman he was having an affair with, didn't know he was married, and she was expecting a baby too."

"Oh, shit!" The moment the words came from Joel's mouth, Kennedy snapped her head up to look at him. His eyes were wide, and his cheeks had even gone a bit red. This was why she never told this story—especially to someone she didn't know.

"Anyway, Chase and I are four months apart in age."

"So, Chase is your half-brother on your father's side."

"Yes. Max is my full-blooded brother, born after my mother somehow was convinced to take my dad back, even though he'd had a child with another woman. I hold a grudge about that."

"You don't like Max?"

Kennedy pressed her hands flat to the top of the table. "I love Max. In fact, we are very tight. I don't like what my father did to my mother. No woman deserves less than one hundred percent of your attention if you tell her you love her. Affairs are brutal, dishonest, and completely disrespectful. And to take a man back, after he's done something like that to you, that's disrespectful to yourself," she bit out the words harshly.

For whatever reason, that hadn't seemed to frighten him, because he covered her hands with his to comfort her.

Kennedy looked at their pile of hands, then looked up at him.

He smiled at her again. "You don't have to share this with me if you don't want to. I didn't realize..."

"This is my story. People think I'm stuck up and snooty, and this is some of it. So, I might as well tell it all to you, so you know who I really am. I mean, we're going to be neighbors. You might as well know why I'm like I am."

He nodded slowly but didn't move his hands until she pulled hers out from under his.

"Max is a year younger than me—and Chase. After Max was born, Mom kicked Dad out. To his credit, he kept me, Max, and Chase together as much as he could, so we were tight-knit. Then he married Leah years later, and they had Paige."

"How much later?"

"Paige is twenty-six. She's a baby in my eyes. A yoga instructor, firm in her convictions, and she will love your style of eating. She's a vegan by day and a carnivore and Oreo eater in the dark."

That drew a full-bellied laugh from Joel who held up his hand until he was done. "I'm sorry. I'm so sorry."

Kennedy couldn't help but laugh too. "It's funny. I'll admit that." She sucked in a cleansing breath. "Paige is one of the lights of my life. She's amazing. Actually, both of my brothers are too. It's just that I hate to watch Chase drive around in my money," she admitted.

The waiter returned with their sizzling platters of fajitas and set them down in front of them. They both agreed to continue to drink just water, and he refilled their glasses.

Joel picked up his fork and stabbed a piece of chicken, holding it in front of his lips as he blew on it. "Do you talk to your dad?" he asked before he took a cautious bite.

"Yes. What he did to my mother was wrong, and for that, I'll never forgive him. But he did right by all of us. He's not a bad man. A little mixed up some times, but he's a good guy. He's raised Paige nearly single-handedly, and she turned out okay."

"What happened to her mother?"

Kennedy sipped her water again before she took on that part of the story. "She was killed by a drunk driver when Paige was seven. She had just dropped her off with me at my job back then. I worked at the GAP at the mall. Paige and I were going to watch a movie, and then I'd take her home, because I was some hot thing with a car—that my daddy bought me out of guilt, I'm sure. But it was supposed to be our special sister night, and the first night they were letting me drive Paige anywhere."

She watched as Joel set his fork down and gave her all of his attention.

"On her way home from the mall, some guy hit her head on. He'd been on a bender after losing his job."

"I'm so sorry," his words were soft and heartfelt.

"Thank you. Things were different after that. I spent a lot more time at my dad's to help with Paige, at my mother's suggestion. We all doted on her and took care of her. My dad stepped up and was mother and father, and Paige is an amazing woman."

"I think my relationship with my brother is the one thing I cherish the most. I love his wife and his kids. It's good to appreciate your siblings."

Kennedy picked up her fork and let her shoulders ease again. Taking a piece of chicken, she ate it before picking back up the conversation, to let the air settle. "My siblings are my life, and then my business."

"The GAP, huh? You've always been a fashion girl?"

"Since I toted around my first Holly Hobbie purse," she said with a laugh, that warranted another from Joel as well.

She took another bite of her chicken and eased into the calm that he brought to her by just being there. This was dangerous territory, she thought. As he sat there, and they now shared casual conversation, she realized she could easily fall for this good-looking man. But having him next door all the time would be a distraction, and if it went bad, he'd still be next door.

She should just appreciate the friendship and the nice meal. That would be the smart thing to do.

CHAPTER 11

hough the meal had been focused on eating well, when Joel had seen the table across the patio from them eating fried ice cream, he had to have some. Somehow, he'd convinced Kennedy to share in the indulgence.

When the tab was paid, and they were both laughing about the sugar they'd consumed, they started back to their end of the block.

"I didn't want to do this," Kennedy admitted as she adjusted the strap of her purse on her shoulder. "But I'm glad I did."

"You don't like me?" Joel gripped his chest as if it pained him.

Kennedy let out a giggle.. "I like you just fine. I just didn't think it would be as nice as it was, especially since you were expecting the story of my family."

"Momentarily twisted, but it sounds like it all worked out."

"Momentarily twisted. I guess you're right. When you think about the fact it was twisted for only a few years, we do okay now."

"As my mother would always remind me, you're an adult much longer than you're a kid. So as long as you're all well-adjusted adults, I guess you're doing okay."

"I guess so."

When they crossed the street and finally stood on the sidewalk between their two properties, silence fell between them. Joel wasn't sure what he was supposed to do now. Did he just say, see ya tomorrow, or was he supposed to hug her? Maybe this was why he avoided dating.

He took a breath to speak, and found that they had something to say at the same time. "This was nice," he said.

"Thank you for dinner," she said.

The shared another laugh. Then Kennedy held out her hand to shake his. That at least gave him a lead.

He took her hand and shook it, but with their proximity it was easy to pull her into a friendly hug.

Her arms came around his neck, and he knew it was the right move. She was at ease with the hug.

Then, as they pulled from the embrace, their cheeks brushed. In one moment their eyes met as the intent went from walking away to something else. In time, he'd never know who decided on the next move. It was as mutual as talking at the same time.

Her lips came to his, and his embrace on her tightened. They were kissing on the sidewalk, and God, he couldn't even feel his feet. Her scent enveloped him, and much like the polish she wore that bore her name, he was sure the scent was signature too.

Kennedy's fingers brushed through is hair at the back of his neck, and it shot a shiver of need through him as her mouth opened to his.

This wasn't a small and friendly kiss. He'd thought about it, but did it mean she had too?

When they broke, they stood connected, their foreheads pressed to one another's.

Kennedy let out a breath. "Wow."

"Yeah," Joel agreed, equally breathless.

"That might have been a huge mistake."

He hadn't seen that opinion coming. "Nope. Mistakes don't feel that good."

Kennedy took a small step back to distance them. "We're neighbors. Business neighbors. I shouldn't be kissing my neighbor."

Joel closed his eyes and shook his head. "Actually, I don't think you should not be kissing your neighbor. That was really nice."

She adjusted the strap on her purse again, and he realized that she used it as an aide when she was uncomfortable. "Are you okay to drive? I should be getting home."

"I'm just fine," he assured her.

Kennedy turned to walk between the buildings toward her car, and Joel felt the need for one more moment. He reached for her hand to stop her progress, and she turned.

"Just for the record. I don't think it was a mistake at all. I'll see you tomorrow."

Her eyes had gone wide for a moment, but when she turned to walk away, he stood still. He'd give her the moment to gather herself and head home. Obviously she was a woman who gave a lot of thought to all the things she did. At that moment, he hoped she'd give him some thought—but not too much. What they'd shared could be ruined if given too much thought.

When she pulled from the parking lot behind her building, she gave him a small wave, and drove off. Then, Joel walked between the buildings and to his truck. He checked that he'd locked the door to the tap house, and then opened the door to his truck.

Starting the engine, he turned the radio from country to hair band rock. He didn't want to chance that some song would take him down the sentimental path. This moment needed to be appreciated for what it was—a beginning. Either he and the woman next door had just started something that could become hot and heavy, or they built on a friendship that was started over dinner when she shared her family secrets with him. Maybe they started a forever thing, or maybe she would hate him now and never speak to him again.

As one song ended, KISS opened their ballad to Beth. Well, changing the station hadn't helped. He backed out of the parking lot and headed home to the lyrics of sweetly blowing off your love to hang with the boys.

His thoughts quickly drew back to Kennedy. What kind of music did she listen to? Immediately he'd peg her for Bach, but something told him the pink, though it ran deep into who she was, was a candy coating. What did the former GAP employee, big sister, fierce business owner listen to when she was in the shower or driving home from work?

He'd find out, he promised himself. He didn't want what happened between them to be lost. He wanted more—maybe forever—with the neighbor next door.

*a*t the first stop light, Kennedy turned the radio in her car to smooth—wordless—jazz. She didn't need Michael Bublé or Harry Connick Jr. messing with her already spinning head. She drove a block before she changed the jazz to hair band rock and KISS finished singing Beth and Ozzy started singing to Mama that he was coming home.

Seriously, she just wanted something to soothe her mind, and music wasn't getting the job done.

At the next stoplight she started a podcast for women business owners. There would be no gaining insight into what they were telling her tonight, but at least they could be the mind-numbing voices in her car drowning out her own—the ones that were talking her out of kissing Joel again.

It wasn't until she pulled into her driveway and waited for the garage door to rise after she'd pressed the button, that she realized she'd enjoyed the kiss. Or at least, that had been her final verdict. The entire drive had been her head mixing up the enjoyment of it with what it meant. It meant they were attracted to one another, they'd enjoyed their evening, and they finished it with a kiss.

A freaking hot kiss.

Kennedy pulled into the garage and let the door close her in. Resting her head against the back of the seat she let her eyes close, and she recreated the kiss in her mind.

Would it be so bad to kiss the neighbor? It wasn't like he'd asked her for forever. He'd asked her to dinner. He'd kissed her, and she'd kissed him back. She'd tangled her fingers in his hair. She'd let their tongues meet, which meant it wasn't just a little kiss.

Heat filled her cheeks and Kennedy let out a laugh in her car.

"Oh, girl, what are you going to do?"

She laughed again as she gathered her items from the passenger seat, opened the car door, and stepped out into the garage that was lit by only one light bulb, as the other had long ago burnt out.

Taking the two wooden steps to the door, she pushed in the code to unlock it, then entered into her laundry room/mud room. She dropped her belongings on the dryer, kicked off her shoes, stepped over the laundry pile on the floor, and maneuvered around the box of items she needed to give away which had found permanent residency in the doorway. There was the stench of stale dishes in the sink, and she decided to tend to those before she even changed her clothes. Her grandmother's voice always crept into her head when her kitchen wasn't spotless—and that was always.

As she scrubbed the dishes and put them in the empty dishwasher, she realized that dinner with Joel had been the first decent meal she'd had in a week. Looking at the cereal and oatmeal bowls that dirtied her kitchen, she didn't abide by his rule of eating only things he could pronounce.

She filled the dishwasher with soap and started the machine. Then she washed out the sink and cleaned down the counters. Pulling the trash from the can, she tied up the bag and carried it to the garage to dump into the can.

On her way back into the house, she threw the laundry into the washer, and carried the box to her car, so that she could drop it off the next day at Goodwill. In another laundry basket, she piled her high heels into it to take them back to her bedroom. She'd spent too much money on them to just kick them in a pile in the laundry room.

When she walked into her bedroom she stopped and dropped the basket. A wave of emotion washed over her, and she just wanted to cry.

Her bed was unmade, and water glasses crowded her nightstand. There were piles of clothes on her floor, workout and lounging clothes, and a chair in the corner housed all of her dry cleaning.

One kiss from a man and her eyes were opened wide to how lonely and depressed she'd been. This was how she lived when she was alone. Her store was bright and pink and tidy. When she was at work her head was filled with ideas and goals to crush. At work, she was sophisticated, proper, and God—she was clean and tidy, but whoever she was at home was pathetic. When was the last time she'd even had someone over to her house?

Paige—Paige was the last person to be in her home and that was nearly a month ago.

Kennedy pressed her fingers to her lips, walked to her bed, and dropped. She was lonely. She'd let herself become some hermit who lived in the fantasy of her job.

Tears began to roll down her cheeks, and she brushed them away. Her mother had gone through this when her father married Leah. She had to assume her mother went through it many times, but Kennedy had been too young to remember.

Well, this wasn't going to do. No, she wasn't going to live some pathetic life where she poured everything she was into her business and let her personal life suffer. She deserved pink and tidy everywhere she went. And she deserved to be kissed by good-looking men in work boots who smelled like lumber.

Kennedy wiped away the final tears, stood and marched to the bathroom. She piled her hair on the top of her head and secured it with a band. With her foot, she kicked the dirty clothes that were flung across the floor into a pile, choosing a pair of leggings and a tank top to replace the dress she had on, she changed her clothes and began an assault on her house to clean it and get it back in shape. All the while knowing she owed Joel a thank you for the attention he'd given her. It was pathetic, and she owned up to that. She'd spent so much time running her business, worrying about her mother and father and her siblings, she'd forgotten to worry about herself.

She hadn't anticipated an awakening of this sort, but she was glad to have it.

CHAPTER 13

*K*ennedy's car was parked out behind her store when Joel pulled into the lot. He put his truck in park and sat there for a moment, looking up at the window where he knew at some point during the day he'd see Kennedy looking out.

Then, as if he'd summoned her to the window, she was there, and she smiled.

He'd fretted over the morning, about seeing her again. He didn't know what to expect after she'd driven away. The feelings had been hot for a moment, but the message he'd received was that she'd regretted the kiss after. It hadn't helped him sleep, but he'd decided he'd let her lead the way.

He stepped out of his truck and gave her a wave. In return, she held up her coffee pot and nodded her head toward her back door. This was an invitation.

Joel reached for his coffee cup, which was full from home, but he'd take the invitation she was offering.

As he approached the back step, the door opened. There, standing before him, dressed in pink from head to toe, was the woman whose image had kept him up all night.

Her hair was in a tight bun at the nape of her neck, and delicate pearls dangled from her ears. Joel knew nothing about dresses, except the one she had on, that was cut low in the front and wrapped around her, tied to the side, fit her like a glove, and he was enjoying the sight of her curves.

Kennedy met him eye to eye in her heels, which matched the dress, of course. A band of pearls graced her delicate wrists, and her pink-painted fingers wrapped around the handle of the coffee pot.

This was hands down the best morning he'd had in a very long time.

"Mornin'," he managed after having taken his time to appreciate the woman before him.

"Fresh coffee. Can I interest you in some?" Her voice shook, and he found it endearing.

Joel lifted his mug. "Just filled up as I left the house this morning, but thanks."

She gave him a quick nod and replaced the pot under the maker as Joel stepped inside fully and shut the door behind him.

Kennedy had paused at the counter, and he was sure a brush off was coming. One that was well formulated and thought through all night long. Maybe he'd stall that for a moment, if he could manage it.

Joel set his coffee mug on the counter, and moved in behind her. Bracing his hands on the counter on either side of her, he pressed his lips to her exposed neck, and felt as she eased back against him. The hum she let out vibrated under his lips.

No, there wasn't going to be a brush off today, he thought as she turned to him and wrapped her arms around his neck. This time she took the initiative to kiss him, and this kiss started where the other had left off.

Joel's hands came to her hips, and her fingers wrapped in his hair. He had to keep reminding himself that this was only their second kiss, and his hands needed to remain firmly on her hips. One false move and this was game over.

Tongues danced and their bodies pressed against one another's until the atmosphere in the room was nearly suffocating. Then came a noise from the doorway to the showroom. Someone had cleared their throat, and when he and Kennedy broke from their kiss—or from their heated making out—there were three women standing there, with wide eyes and stupid grins, staring at them.

Two of the women he had met, who worked for Kennedy. The other he didn't know, but she had the biggest grin of them all.

The woman who he hadn't yet met held up a hand. "Please don't stop on account of us. We could watch this aaall daaay," she said, dragging out the words.

Joel watched as Kennedy's shoulders pressed back, and the air in the room stirred differently now.

The women must have noticed it too, as they all turned and scurried off, giggling like little girls.

Joel picked up his coffee, and rested his hip against the counter. "Guess we're not hiding this very well, are we? Not that I'd want to hide it."

Kennedy spun, the look in her eyes wasn't warm now, and Joel eased his hip off the counter and stood erect in front of her.

"Maybe you should go now."

He watched her for another moment, hoping the disdain that had darkened her eyes would lift, but no luck. Her lips pursed, and he realized the lipstick wasn't there anymore. Taking the back of his hand over his lips, he noted most of it was now on his skin.

"What time are you done today?" he asked, hoping to move past the very awkward silence that had come between them.

"I'm very busy today."

"That wasn't my question."

Kennedy picked up her mug and filled it with coffee before

turning back to him. "My last client arrives at five-thirty. She tries on everything I have, so I don't suppose I'll be done until well after six-thirty."

"You'll need to eat then. I'll watch for you."

With that he turned and walked out of the store. He wasn't going to let her make up an excuse to not be with him. He wouldn't press the issue of the kiss or what they thought might be happening. No, tonight he'd make sure she had a nice dinner and that they let the air clear. Surely those three women would want some gossip, but he'd have to let her handle them.

As it was, when he turned the corner, there were three men looking at him much the same way the women had looked at Kennedy. They had seen them through the window, and now they too wanted the story.

Joel wondered if anyone would be productive today.

CHAPTER 14

*K*ennedy watched Joel walk toward the men who were audibly giving him a hard time over what they'd seen. She couldn't make out the words, but she watched as he shook his head at them while they patted him on the back.

As he walked through the back door of the tap house, he looked up to the window and caught her looking back at him. He offered a smile, and for some reason that calmed her. It told her they were in this together, and he wasn't just a kiss and tell kind of guy.

"Kennedy, you'd better get out here," her sister's voice rang through the store forcing her to close her eyes and take a breath.

Well, Joel might not kiss and tell—she hoped—but she supposed that was exactly what she was about to do. There was no way those three women were going to let her off the hook.

With her coffee between her hands, she walked out to the showroom, poised as the Kennedy at work would be. She walked straight to the stool behind the counter, perched atop it, and crossed her legs all the while never letting go of her mug.

Paige carried a chair over for Cara to sit in, and Hillary stood at the counter with her elbows atop it, and her face rested in her hands.

Paige joined Hillary in the same pose, as if they were little kids waiting for a bedtime story.

"Spill it, sis," Paige demanded, and Kennedy thought she looked so young at that moment.

"There is nothing to tell."

Hillary stood and flipped her hair over her shoulder. "Bull! Now, that wasn't a scene where he stumbled into you and your faces got caught together. That was a fully engaged kiss, with tongue, and hands, and it said a lot. What it really said was that wasn't the first kiss. No, this one had some comfort to it."

Paige turned her head to look at Hillary. "You put a lot of thought into that."

"I did," Hillary admitted before turning her attention back to Kennedy. "Now, give us the deets."

Kennedy sipped from her mug. "He took me to dinner last night after I tested some beers they're going to be bringing in to the tap room."

Paige narrowed her eyes on her sister. "You drank beer."

"I drink beer."

Paige let out a low hum. "Were any of them worthy?"

"There was a coffee and chocolate infused one that I..."

Cara cleared her throat and all heads turned toward her. "Are you kidding me? You're going to describe the beer and not the kiss with the hunky guy in the steel-toed boots?"

As she rubbed her enlarged stomach, the other three women laughed. Leave it to the woman who could go into labor at any moment to be the one who wanted the saucy details.

Kennedy let out a breath. "I went to dinner with him. We talked. We walked back here, and we kissed."

Paige pressed her fingers to her lips. "You kissed? Like one kiss?"

"One kiss," Kennedy admitted and then thought better of it. "One long, hot, intense kiss."

That warranted a howl from Paige and a round of laughter that heated Kennedy's cheeks. God it felt good to talk like this with her friends.

But a moment later, the fun was over. Her first client walked through the door, and after her followed a tiny dog, which Kennedy wasn't fond of. But the woman spent obscene amounts of money with her, so the dog got a special bowl to eat from and Hillary would take her for a walk when the big decisions were being made as to how many outfits the woman would be taking home.

"Good morning, Phyllis," Kennedy hopped off the stool and turned on her charm. It was time to pay the rent, she thought as everyone scattered to do their jobs.

⁓

JEFF thew the roll of blueprints onto the makeshift table, and the four men gathered around. However, this morning they didn't dive right into the work for the day. All eyes were on Joel.

"Are we not going to get started?" he asked as he sipped luke-warm coffee from his travel mug.

Oliver folded his arms in front of him. "You're kissing the snooty girl next door, dude. Please explain."

"She's not snooty," he bit the words out and that got a chuckle from his brother. "I'm serious."

"We know. It's a posh store, it just comes across that way. You're usually not an ass-hat either, but you own a bar."

"Tap house," he corrected and Jeff laughed again.

"Just tell us what's going on and maybe we'll leave you alone."

The maybe was hypothetical he knew. There was no way

around it. Nothing would be getting done if he didn't say something.

"I had her taste some beers last night, and then we went to dinner. We walked back here, we kissed, and then went home."

Craig clicked his tongue. "Whose home?"

"You're a child," Joel picked up the rolled up blueprints and began to spread them out.

"I'm a child with a dirty mind. Without proper details, I'll make my own," Craig added.

Joel took one more sip from his coffee and looked at the men that surrounded him. He trusted them with his life, so what would a little gossip hurt to get them all to work.

"Fine. I kissed her last night. It was awesome. But she went one way and I went the other. In fact, when we parted I was fairly sure she wouldn't speak to me again."

His brother shook his head. "It didn't look like she was ignoring you this morning."

"I'm as shocked as you are. When I got here, she invited me over for coffee. I hurried over. When she turned around, I kissed her neck, and then rest was what you saw, and what the girls in her store saw."

Oliver threw a pencil in his direction. "Oh, shit! You're town gossip now."

"Well, that's not what I want," Joel said as he put the pencil behind his ear. "I want her to respect me. I like her."

"You're not exactly a hot shot in the relationship department."

"I do okay. I had one good go. I'm up for seeing how this one would work out too." And as he said it, he knew it to be true. He didn't just want something casual or something that might fizzle out. He was truly interested in Kennedy, and it mattered.

CHAPTER 15

That little dog yapped for three hours. Kennedy's jaw hurt from grinding her teeth and pressing a smile to her lips. But with every outfit that she pulled out for the woman there was an "awww," and an "oooh."

The rack where Kennedy hung the items of interest was nearly full, and the woman wasn't done. Casually, she rolled a second rack into the room and continued to appease the woman, and the dog.

In the fourth hour, Kennedy and Cara bagged up the outfits the woman had purchased. The bill had come to nearly three thousand dollars, which was more than the woman had ever spent in the store. But, with a toothy smile, the woman handed over her credit card and Kennedy ran the amount.

She and Hillary carried the bags to the woman's car as Cara helped a customer who had walked in to browse.

As they watched the woman and her dog turn the corner, Hillary and Kennedy leaned against one another.

"She's a lot of work," Kennedy said on an exhausted breath.

"She makes your rent monthly," Hillary reminded her as she blew a stray curl from face.

"That she does. Where do you suppose she wears all those nice clothes?"

Hillary shrugged. "I'm guessing she has a house with spare bedrooms that have been turned into closets, and the clothes are just on display."

"Do you suppose that dog has its own room too?"

Hillary wrapped her arm around Kennedy's shoulders. "No doubt. And it probably has a bed bigger than yours."

"I'm starving."

Hillary led Kennedy back toward the store. "I'll order in. Chinese?"

"Too much sodium."

"You can drink more water and put your feet up the rest of the day."

"Get extra egg rolls."

Joel and Jeff hurried toward the dress shop just as Kennedy and Hillary opened the door.

"Is there a fire?" Kennedy asked as Jeff reached the door just as Hillary was going to open it.

"We came to see the customer that just walked in," Joel said and Kennedy's heart rate kicked up just by the way he looked at her, and then she registered what he'd said.

Kennedy narrowed her gaze on him. "Did your mother just come into my store?"

He nodded slowly. "I told her to make an appointment, but I think she wanted to check it out first."

"I don't think I'm ready to meet your mother."

"Too late," he whispered and with his hand at the small of her back, he led her through the door.

"Oh, my goodness," the woman in the purse section placed her hand on her chest. "There's my boys."

Kennedy stood near the counter and watched the interaction. Both boys bent to kiss their mother on the cheek. She showed them a purse she was looking at, and they both gave their gracious opinions. Then, Joel turned to Kennedy and nodded for her to join them. With a small shove from Hillary, Kennedy pushed back her shoulders and turned up the pink painted smile on her lips.

"Mom, this is Kennedy Devereaux. She owns the store," Joel said.

Kennedy held out her hand to the woman. "It's a pleasure to meet you, Mrs. Kingsley."

"It's June," she offered as she shook Kennedy's hand. "This is a beautiful store. Joel said he knew I would like it. And aren't you as beautiful as he said you were."

Kennedy could feel the heat rise in her cheeks, and it didn't help that Joel was staring at her with a stupid grin on his face. "That was very sweet of him."

Jeff moved in again and kissed his mother on the cheek. "We have to get back. Stop by when you're done."

"I'll do that," she said.

Joel kissed her other cheek. "Have fun." Then he looked at Kennedy as if he might kiss her goodbye too.

Perhaps the piercing stare she was giving him warned him not to make a move. Instead, he smiled at her sweetly and said goodbye to the girls as he walked out of the store.

"He's fond of you, my Joel," June said as she picked up another purse. "You have exquisite things here."

Usually customers didn't frazzle Kennedy as much as June Kingsley did. Even the woman with the yappy dog didn't make her nervous. But this was somehow different. Joel had told his mother about her, even before they'd kissed.

"Thank you," she finally managed. "A few of the handbags I've designed, and most of the custom costume jewelry pieces as well." Kennedy angled to gesture to the table in the center of the room.

"I'm going to look at them next. I saw a bracelet the moment I walked in. And that pink on your nails. I'll need a bottle of that for sure."

And hadn't Joel said that, too?

"I can set up the showing room for you if you'd like to look at clothes as well. I just had a client, and it would just take me a few minutes."

June rested a hand on Kennedy's arm. "I'll make an appointment for that. In fact, if you don't mind, I'd like to bring my sister as well. She does love pretty things."

"That would be delightful."

"Now, which of these purses did you design?"

June Kingsley made an appointment for the following Tuesday afternoon, and she would bring her sister. She carried out a pink bag with twine handles, and inside was a *Kennedy Devereaux Designs* purse, scarf, and on her wrist one of the newest bracelets that Kennedy had made. The pink polish that had been wrapped in tissue paper was a gift from Kennedy.

"The driver with our lunch approaches," Hillary said as she looked at her phone.

Kennedy pressed her hand to her grumbling stomach, and the other to her chest as she watched Joel's mother put her bag into her car and then walk to toward the tap house. There was something about a man's relationship with his mother that could make a girl's knees go weak, and Joel and his mother had that relationship.

A small part of her didn't want to be interested in Joel Kingsley, but that was a control factor and Kennedy knew it. Being interested in a man meant that her attention would be split between her business and him—and she was all business. The thought took her back to the night she'd had cleaning her house, because she had been all business, and she'd forgotten to be Kennedy.

Now she'd met Joel's mother, and it had made him even more

endearing. He came from good stock, and she could say that with conviction after having seen how both Joel and Jeff treated her.

If she carried on with him, she'd be in good hands too.

Her mind was brought back to the present as Cara clutched her stomach and let out groan like nothing Kennedy had ever heard.

"Are you okay?" she hurried to Cara behind the counter.

"My water just broke."

CHAPTER 16

*T*he Chinese food arrived just as Kennedy made the call to Cara's husband and Hillary ran outside to pull her car up front.

Kennedy tipped the driver, and then helped Cara to Hillary's car. She would take Cara to the hospital where her husband would meet them.

As soon as Hillary pulled from the curb, Kennedy noticed Joel running from the front of the tap room toward her.

"Is everything okay? Is Cara okay? Are you okay?"

His questions came at her quickly, without a breath between them and Kennedy found that she couldn't answer him. Every one of her senses was overwhelmed. From the moment his mother had walked into her store until the moment she stood alone on the street, the smell of Chinese food wafting out the door, she'd been immersed in nonstop chatter and panic.

Tears began to choke her, and instinct told her to turn around, go back inside, and lock the door. But that wasn't going to do her any good. Her lips began to tremble and Joel stepped in closer.

He took her hands in his and made sure their eyes met. "Cara's okay?"

"Her water broke."

A smile formed on his lips and it brought a calm to her as he pulled her into his arms. "Well then, all of that panic is a good thing. There's a baby on the way."

The pure joy and hint of excitement that filled his voice made the tears break free. Kennedy didn't cry in front of people, and here she was, wrapped in the arms of a man who was still a stranger, even though she'd been kissing him, on the street. It went against everything she thought she was.

"C'mon, let's get you inside," he said. "Gladys will probably come over any minute to see what's going on."

He was a quick study, she thought. If Gladys caught any of the exchanges in the past four minutes, she'd be looking for the gossip. Kennedy needed to pull herself together.

Joel followed her inside the store, but let her walk to her office alone. She took a moment to wipe her eyes, and then she fixed her makeup and sprayed the few loose strands of hair back into place.

When she passed the break room, she noticed Joel at the table with the bag of Chinese food. He'd made her a plate and had pulled a bottle of water from the refrigerator.

"I know you have more clients coming, so eat your lunch. It's already past lunchtime." He stood and pulled out the chair for her.

"You didn't have to do all of this. I'm just emotional because Cara's baby is coming." That wasn't the whole truth, but she'd be damned if she told him how twisted up she was just watching his mother walk over to their tap room to see what her boys were working on.

"Believe it or not, men get giddy over new babies too. I remember when my sister-in-law went into labor, Jeff put a staple into my boot. Thank goodness for steel toes," he laughed.

"I don't look stupid to you?"

"Dear Lord, why would you think that? How exciting, right? There's a baby coming. Everything will be different."

Everything was different, and at that moment it washed through her. She moved from her chair, and nearly leapt into Joel's lap. Cupping his face in her hands, she pulled him to her and kissed him.

His hands came around her and held her into place on his lap as she deepened the kiss that had stirred her up more, but calmed all the energy that had set her into tears in the first place.

Once again, their kiss was interrupted by someone in the doorway clearing their throat.

As they both turned their heads, Paige leaned against the door jamb with her arms folded in front of her. "Have you two gotten any work done today. Or have you just been making out all day?"

There was humor in her voice, and Kennedy wanted to react to that, but Joel's arms around her hadn't given. He wasn't ashamed of what they were doing, and he held her in place.

"What are you doing here?" Kennedy asked.

Paige pulled out a chair and sat down. She looked into the containers on the table and pulled out an egg roll. Taking a bite, she looked at the two of them on one chair.

"Hillary called and said she was taking Cara to the hospital. She thought I should come by and lend you a hand." Paige shifted her eyes to Joel. "Her manners suck. I'm Paige, by the way. Baby sister."

"Joel Kingsley, owner of the tap room next door," he said, his arms still holding Kennedy in place on his lap.

"Nice to meet you." She took another bite of the egg roll and shifted her attention to Kennedy. "I don't have a class until six. I only have what I'm wearing, so if you want me to look the part, I'll need an outfit to wear."

Kennedy stood and took the bottle of water as she walked to

the back room, pulled a jumpsuit from the rack, and carried it back to the break room.

"Are you clean?" she asked Paige, the garment still in her hand.

"I am. I don't teach until six," Paige assured her with a tone of annoyance. "But a jumpsuit?"

"You have the perfect body for it, and it'll look cute with your sandals. Go get changed. My next client comes at two-thirty. By the way, that egg roll had pork in it."

Paige took one more bite of the egg roll and wiped her hands on a napkin before taking the jumpsuit into the back room to change.

Joel pushed the plate toward Kennedy. "Eat. You're running out of time and this is getting cold."

Kennedy sat down, and this time she picked up the chopsticks and moved the food around the plate. "Thank you."

"For what?"

"Rushing over here and calming me down. I would have cried, pulled myself together, and gone on with the day. But I never would have sat down to eat."

"You haven't eaten yet. Take a bite."

Kennedy took a bite, and at that moment she realized just how hungry she was. "Your mother is delightful."

"She said the same about you. She made me promise to go to her house and see the purse you designed."

"She didn't just take it in and show you?"

"This way she gets me over to her house." He picked up the egg roll that Paige hadn't finished and bit into it. "At some point she'll want you to come with me."

"I'll think about it," Kennedy teased as she lifted noodles to her mouth and savored them.

"I'll be waiting for you when you're done tonight."

Before she hadn't thought too much about it, but now she wanted to spend the evening with him.

"I'll come over as soon as I'm done."

Joel stood and pressed a gentle kiss to her lips. "I'll see you soon."

This time he let himself out the back door and disappeared.

Paige walked back into the break room with the jumpsuit on. Kennedy had been right, she had the perfect body for it.

"He's a keeper," Paige said looking out the window over the sink, no doubt watching Joel go back to work.

Kennedy lifted another bite to her mouth. Yes, she thought. Time would tell, but her initial reaction was that he was a keeper.

CHAPTER 17

*T*he call had come at eleven twenty-seven that evening. Melody McEwan had been born.

Kennedy sat up in her bed, still awake after her nice dinner with Joel, and a literal teenage make out session in the back of her car. It had kept her wired, and she was glad there was something to take her mind off the man for just a moment.

"Oh, Kennedy, she's beautiful," Cara boasted. "I think she looks just like Brian. Brian thinks she looks just like me."

Kennedy pressed her hand to her chest. "I can't wait to see her."

"You can come by in the morning. We're allowed visitors at any time."

"I'll be there. Congratulations, Cara. I'm so excited for you."

"Thank you. I'll see you in the morning."

They disconnected and Kennedy lay in her bed, silence and darkness surrounding her. Children had never been on her radar, but there was something that happened to her when friends had them—a softness took over.

Maybe she'd sold herself short thinking she didn't want kids. But past relationships had proven to her that she wasn't the marrying type, and if she couldn't commit to a man, how could she commit to a child?

Could she commit herself to Joel?

Now, wide awake, Kennedy sat up in her bed. She'd been kissing the man for two days, it wasn't time to think about commitment. He hadn't even made a move that told her that he wanted more than a kiss.

Oh, who was she kidding? She'd met his mother. The man had just been raised right. He would probably keep his hands off of her until she made the first move in that department. But she wasn't thinking about moving to the next stages of dating. She was full on thinking marriage and babies. That wasn't like her, and she was smart enough to. know that this was all brought on by Cara having a baby. It was momentary.

Kennedy and her siblings didn't talk about marriage and forever because they'd seen that it didn't work. One man and his actions had proved to them all that some could go all-in to a relationship, and some couldn't commit at all. What if she was the one that couldn't commit? Her family's story wasn't anything like Joel's.

Still, she thought of him as she arranged her pillows and rested her head back on them. The kisses after dinner that led them to the back of her car resonated in her rapid heart rate that still hadn't calmed.

Joel Kingsley stirred her up, and it had been a long time since someone had done that.

She let the memory of his fingers in her hair, and his body pressed to hers carry her into sleep where she dreamed of him. In her dream she let the fantasy fulfill itself. They kissed, they made love, they married, and they had children. All the while, they continued to look at each other as if they were starstruck in one another's presence.

Could reality be represented by a lust-filled dream?

Kennedy rose early the next morning, and though she hadn't had her usual amount of sleep, she was rested. She decided new attitudes deserved some attention. Her house was still clean from her binge cleaning, and there was enough room in front of her TV to do some yoga.

Paige had been begging her to take one of her classes, but Kennedy didn't want to make time for it. There was no other way to address it. Paige, being the persistent one, had given her an online membership to some YouTube star's yoga site, and Kennedy decided this was the morning to try it.

She managed twenty minutes before she realized she wasn't going to be able to move again for a week.

"I have to do this more often," she groaned as she rolled from her mat and got ready for the day.

An hour later, she was driving up in front of the hospital with a bag she'd had for the occasion sitting in the passenger seat.

Kennedy parked the car and noticed Hillary walking toward the building. She called to her and they walked in together.

Cara was nursing when they walked into the room. Brian had gone home for a shower and a change of clothes.

Kennedy and Hillary sat down at Cara's bedside and watched as the little girl's hand wrapped around her mother's finger.

Hillary sniffed back tears. "Cara, she's perfect."

"She is, isn't she? I cannot believe how in love I am with her. I mean, there is no other feeling like it."

Kennedy watched as Cara finished nursing and handed the baby to Hillary, who quickly sat down in her chair as if she were afraid to drop her.

Those stirrings from the night before now spun in Kennedy's stomach and threatened to make her sick. She wondered if Cara noticed when she drew her attention away from the baby.

"What did you bring?"

Kennedy picked up the bag to her side and handed it to Cara.

"Oh my goodness," she laughed as she pulled out the onesie. "Is this *Kennedy Pink*?"

"I had it custom-made. There are four of them to get her through the first year. She had to look stylish."

Cara held it up to show Hillary the monogram in center of the fabric.

Hillary looked up at Kennedy. "Do you want to hold her?"

The rate of Kennedy's heart sped up. "I don't think so."

Cara let out a sigh. "She's not going to break and you're not going to hurt her."

Hillary stood and carried the baby over to her, setting her gently in her arms.

Melody wrapped her hand around her finger and a tear rolled down Kennedy's cheek. She laughed when Melody yawned and Kennedy's mind went straight to the man in the work boots that had been playing havoc with her mind. Maybe, just maybe she could have something as perfect as a man and a baby in her life. Would that be so impossible?

CHAPTER 18

*K*ennedy took a few extra minutes on her drive in and stopped to get fancy coffees for herself and Hillary. The store could run with two, but three always made it easier. It would be a while before Cara would be back—if she'd be back. Kennedy was prepared for her to choose motherhood over her job.

Hillary's car was already parked behind the store and a big truck followed Kennedy into the lot, blocking her exit. As she climbed from her car, coffees in hand, Jeff hurried out of the back of the tap house.

"Can I help you in with those?" he asked as he approached.

"No, I'm fine."

"We're unloading materials. I know this blocks you both in. Will you be okay with that for a couple hours or so?"

Kennedy looked at the big truck. "We should be fine. It's just for a few hours, right?"

"Yeah. We'll get him off loaded and out of here as soon as possible. Gladys moved her car to make her deliveries, but he followed you in before I could get to you."

"We should be fine," she said again.

"Great. I appreciate it." Jeff hurried off and Kennedy waited another moment hoping that Joel would pop his head out, and he'd say hello. But he never did emerge, so she carried the coffees inside.

The moment she walked through the door, she noticed the bouquet of flowers on the table as Hillary walked into the room. Kennedy held out a coffee to her, and she took it.

"What are the flowers? Are they for Cara?" she asked.

Hillary shook her head. "Gladys just delivered them. They're for you. There's a card."

Kennedy walked to the table and pulled the card from the bouquet. Setting down her coffee, she opened the small envelope.

Good Morning! Love, Joel

"You have the stupidest grin on your face," Hillary teased. "Are they from Joel?"

"Yes."

"God, you're lucky. He's the package, Ken. Good-looking, loves his mama, and he's motivated. You just cannot go wrong there."

No, she was sure Hillary was right. But, it was new, and newness always wore off.

The bell above the door in the other room chimed and Hillary and Kennedy exchanged looks. It was time for the day to begin.

Kennedy worked her magic for the next three hours, showing women with open pocketbooks fashionable looks from her last trips to Paris and New York. As she tidied the room, Hillary walked in with the store phone in her hand.

"It's your dad. He says he's been calling you for an hour." She handed the phone to Kennedy and went back out to the showroom.

"Dad, what's wrong?" she began the conversation. There was no reason for him to call her on the store line if it wasn't urgent. He knew how she worked.

"I need a ride. Can you get here in the next hour?"

She looked up into the full length mirror and saw the look of disdain on her face. "Are you kidding me? I'm working."

"Yep, and you're my only hope. You're self-employed and I need a ride."

"You have a son who is self-employed and drives cars for a living."

"He's got a fare, as he put it."

"Your other son and your other daughter are also self-employed."

"Kennedy, I need a ride. Pick me up within the hour please." He didn't even finish the phone call, or give any more excuses. He disconnected the call and left Kennedy standing there looking at her reflection in the mirror.

She hurried back out to the counter and brought up the schedule. It was one o'clock, and she didn't have any more private appointments. Anything that came up, Hillary could handle. But she still wasn't happy with her father.

Maybe she could hire an Uber to pick him up and take him where he needed to go. The only problem was, she didn't know where it was he was so urgently taking off to.

Forget it, she thought as she explained the situation to Hillary. Maybe she needed a few moments alone with her father to give him a piece of her mind. She wasn't in business for herself to have others tell her when she could or couldn't work. This wasn't how it worked.

After righting the back room, because she felt as if she needed a few more moments to process what was going on, she grabbed her purse and headed out to her car. The truck that had pulled in behind her was still parked there. Hadn't Jeff told her it wouldn't be but a few hours?

Now she didn't have time for delays. She pulled the strap of her purse over her shoulder and marched toward the back door of the tap room.

Laying on the floor, just beyond the back door, Joel was under a sink with a wrench in his hand.

"I need that truck moved," she spat out the words and watched as he slowly lifted his head and grinned.

"Hey, lovely. I was thinking about you."

"I need that truck out of the way."

"Did you get something this morning?"

Kennedy let out a long breath. "I don't have time for this."

"Okay, okay." He eased to his feet. "The truck broke down. It'll be another hour or so before the guy gets here with the part they need to fix it."

"Are you kidding me?" Her voice had risen enough Joel retracted a step to keep his distance. "I need to leave now. This is some kind of offense to block in my car like that."

"Jeff said he spoke to you."

"He said it would be a few hours. It's been many more than that."

Joel pulled a set of keys from his pocket. "Take my truck."

"Are you kidding me? I'm not going to drive that."

"It's clean inside, and at this very moment it's your only option."

She hated that he said it that way, because he was right. It was her only option. She could just call her father and tell him to change his plans, but she wouldn't do that. It wasn't like her to completely blow him off, even if it was what she wanted to do.

"I don't know where I'm going and I don't know when I'll be back." She adjusted her purse, and he must have taken that as a sign to walk closer.

"Take my truck and come back when you're done. I'd take you if I didn't have a leaky pipe to tend to."

Kennedy took a breath to calm herself. "My father called and said he needed a ride, and I was the only one able to do it. I'm not happy, and now I have to take your truck." She reached for the keys.

"It's full of gas."

"I'll bring it back the same."

"I didn't mean that. I mean it's ready for you to do whatever you need to do. Call me if you need me."

Joel stepped closer and pressed a kiss to her cheek, and it seemed more intimate than if he'd kissed her on the lips.

Kennedy watched as he pulled back slowly. "Thank you for the flowers. They were lovely."

"A lovely gift for a lovely lady. I'll be here when you get back."

She watched as he turned back to the sink and crawled back under. Hillary's words came back to her—*He's the package. Good-looking, loves his mama, and he's motivated. You just cannot go wrong there.*

*a*fter a few minutes in Joel's truck familiarizing herself with the settings, Kennedy pulled away from the curb and headed toward her father's house.

At a stop light, Kennedy looked around the cab. It was clean, and that didn't hold up to her image of a pickup truck, especially one filled with construction materials in the back.

Guilt then swarmed in her belly. He was going to need his tools, and whatever materials were stowed in the back. The last thing he should have done was lent her his truck.

Her father was standing on his front porch when she pulled up and rolled down the window.

"C'mon," she said as if she were his mother, and he grinned, which only aggravated her more.

He pulled open the back door, slid his suitcase in the back seat, and then climbed up into the cab of the truck. "I expect Chase to drive up in funny trucks and cars, but this one isn't your style."

Kennedy put the truck into drive before he even got his seat-belt on. "Where am I taking you with a suitcase?"

"To the airport."

Kennedy pulled the truck to the side of the road and put it back in park. "The airport? Where are you going?"

A stupid grin formed on her father's lips. "I'm going on a cruise. I have a flight that leaves for Florida in two and a half hours, so move."

"Since when are you going on a cruise?"

"Since this morning. Seriously, Ken, go."

Kennedy put the truck back into drive and headed toward the highway. "Dad, you can't just up and leave on a cruise."

"As it happens, you can. I have the money. I have the time. And I have a more than generous daughter who is taking me to the airport, so I can go on a cruise. But this truck has a story."

She gripped the steering wheel tighter. "It belongs to the guy who is building the tap house next door to my store. They have a truck that was delivering supplies broken down behind my store, so my car is blocked. See, this isn't so convenient."

Her father placed his hand on her shoulder. "And I appreciate your sacrifice even more. Paige wouldn't even take my call."

And with that said, Paige was going to get an earful from Kennedy.

She listened to her father making lists of the things he'd done before leaving, such as stopping his mail and turning off his water. Somewhere he mentioned that Max would check on his place, but wasn't it interesting he couldn't find time to drop their father off, Kennedy thought.

Kennedy pulled up to the drop off zone and stopped. Her father quickly hopped out of the truck and pulled his suitcase out of the back. Kennedy put the truck in park and got out too.

"Where are you really going? You can't just take off," she scolded.

Her father set his suitcase on the ground and pulled a neatly folded piece of paper from his pocket. "You're a lot like your mother. You like details."

She wasn't sure if what he said was a compliment, or a jab.

Kennedy opened the piece of paper and looked at it. "You're going to the Virgin Islands."

"I told you. I'm going on a cruise."

"And you just woke up yesterday and decided you wanted to go?"

"The glory of retirement, sweetheart. Work hard so you can play hard. I hope someday you can lock up shop and just take off for an adventure." He leaned in and kissed her on the cheek. "Thank the guy who let you borrow his truck. It's a nice one. Men who keep their trucks this nice don't just lend them out. He must think you're something special," he said with a smile before turning and walking into the airport.

Kennedy stood beyond the doors for a moment longer thinking about what her father had said. Between the taking off for an adventure and a man liking her enough to lend her his truck, she worked to wrap her head around it all.

It was intriguing to her that when she called her brothers and her sister on her way back to the store, none of them answered. Anger tightened in her chest, and she had to take a few long breaths to ease the tension. So, they didn't answer. They didn't step up. The gracious part of her heart said that they were all so busy being successful, they couldn't take the phone calls. The callous side thought she might lock them all in a tiny room and leave them there.

When she pulled up to the entrance to the parking lot behind the tap house and her building, she noticed the big truck had gone. Her car was now accessible. Hillary's car was still parked next to hers.

Kennedy parked the truck next to the other trucks behind the tap house. As she stepped out, Joel emerged from the back door wiping his hands on a rag.

"Did you get him where he needed to go?" Joel asked as he walked toward her.

Kennedy shut the door and held out Joel's keys. "He decided to take a cruise."

"Just decided?"

"Just decided. He says that's what retirement is about. Getting to decide to go on an adventure."

Joel's brows rose. "Sounds like solid advice. Maybe we should take an adventure."

That tightening was back in her chest. "I don't just run off on adventures."

"Maybe you should someday. How much longer do you have at the store?"

Kennedy looked at her phone for the time. "A few more hours."

"I'll be here until about eight. Jeff has a dance recital to go to. Craig had an appointment downtown to get some paperwork sorted for the licenses. I can't remember what Oliver had to do, but he was going to take off for a few days."

At that moment she felt as if they shared a kindred spirit. Her family had hung her out to dry, and his partners had done the same.

Joel stepped closer to her. "Maybe, if you feel up to it, you could come over when you're done, and we could order in some dinner. I'll be painting."

"You have walls to paint?"

His smile grew wide. "Want to come see?"

Kennedy looked toward her shop. "I'll come when I'm done. I'll bring dinner."

"I like the sound of that," he said as he moved in and pressed a quick kiss to her lips. "Are we still good with all the kissing?"

Her lips twitched as she thought about it. Was he really asking her that? "That's a strange question."

"Is it?" He kissed her quickly again. "Seems to be all I've been thinking about. First kisses and next kisses are an adventure of sorts, aren't they? Maybe your dad was onto something. Our adventure is just a little different." He turned around and walked back through the door.

"I have your keys," she held them in her hand.

"Bring them with you tonight."

She stood there, alone, for a moment. Was he right? Was this her spontaneous adventure?

When Kennedy looked back to her shop, Hillary was in the window smiling. Oh, hell, she thought, she might as well enjoy it then. All adventures eventually came to an end, but they'd be wasted if she didn't find something good in them.

CHAPTER 20

*K*ennedy locked the door to her shop and swiftly climbed into her car. She had told Joel she'd bring dinner, and she had every intention to do so. But first, she was going to stop by home and change her clothes.

She had decided that if she and Joel were having some kind of adventure, she'd like to be part of the tap room. Though she was still worried that it would be like having a bar next door, watching the building next door resurrect into something new was refreshing.

As Kennedy pulled into her driveway, she pushed the button to lift the garage door, and drove in. Because she never got out of her car until the door had closed, she turned off the engine and waited. Then, she opened the car door, took her bags with her, and headed inside.

She smiled as she walked into the laundry room and there wasn't a pile of laundry, shoes, or giveaway items. The house smelled fresh, and the kitchen counters and sink were bare. Yes, this was how a woman who lived alone, and had no one else to make messes should live.

Setting her bag on the chair in the living room, she headed

toward her bedroom. The bed was made and all of her clothes were clean and put away. She caught herself smiling in the mirror over her dresser.

Opening the drawer to the dresser that housed her T-shirts, she pulled out an old one that she'd used to paint in a few times. She then moved to her closet and pulled out a pair of jeans she kept handy for doing yard work. There were holes in the knees and the bottom hem had been cut off and was frayed.

She changed her clothes and moved to the kitchen. Pulling out six bottles of water from the refrigerator, she put them into a thermo bag to keep them cool. Opening her laptop on her counter, she searched for the barbecue restaurant she'd been hungry for, and put an order in online. She'd pick it up on her way back to the tap house.

<hr />

JOEL HAD GONE OUT to his truck to retrieve the bucket from the back. Kennedy's car was missing, and he realized she had his truck keys. As was his practice, the tailgate to the truck was locked, and so was his pickup. Surely she'd just gone to get dinner, as she said she'd bring it back with her. But for now, he was stuck there.

Just as he turned to walk back into the building, Kennedy pulled in beside his truck and turned off her car.

A smile came to his lips instinctively. He'd never been so giddy over seeing a woman in his life. Even the last woman he'd had a relationship with hadn't made him feel the same way.

When she opened her door and swung her legs out, his smile only widened. She was in a pair of old sneakers, ratty jeans, and a T-shirt. Her blonde hair had been braided, and those blue eyes were shaded behind a pair of Ray-Bans. If his heart hadn't started to hammer the moment he'd seen her, he'd have thought she was someone else. Yet, Kennedy could even make casual clothing look sophisticated.

"The bags of food are in the backseat," she said as she pulled a thermo bag from her passenger seat and climbed from the car.

Joel opened the backdoor. "You ordered Frank's? That place is to die for."

"I'm glad you like it." She closed her door with her hip. "I've had a craving for it."

"Do you have my keys?" he asked.

Reaching into her purse, she pulled them out. "You told me to take them. So if you needed them, that's on you."

"It totally is."

Joel took the keys and unlocked his tailgate with his free hand. He retrieved the bucket, set it on the ground, and locked the tailgate again before walking into the building with the food and the bucket.

"Can I help you carry some of that?" Kennedy asked and he shook his head.

"I'm good. Go on in."

Kennedy walked through the back door, and he walked behind her. Just the sight of her in jeans stirred him up. That was a good sign, he thought. She could be different, and if the guys could see her now, they wouldn't think she looked as stuck up as they thought she was.

"This place looks great," she said as she took in the sight of the walls.

Joel set the bucket down. "I think that's the fun part about restorations. One day you have nothing, and then one day it just all comes together. We have some inspections next week, then we can do even more. By the end of next month, you won't even recognize the place."

She turned to him. Her sunglasses rested on top of her head, and those blue eyes sparkled. She had to be the most beautiful woman he had ever laid eyes on.

"You enjoy this, don't you?"

"Of course. Someday we'll sell it and do it all over again."

Her eyes lost their sparkle. "You'll sell it."

"Well, that's the scope of business. We'll run it until someone comes along and wants it."

She folded her arms in front of her and looked around. "I put too much of myself into my business. I can't imagine anyone taking it over."

"If they did, it wouldn't be *Kennedy Devereaux Designs*. But anyone can pour beer."

"But your name is on it."

He nodded. "I'd keep that part." Joel set the bag of food on the makeshift table. "I own a few rental houses too, so when this is done, I'll buy another house to flip. Once it's in your blood, you need projects."

"My brother Max is like that. He likes to flip houses, build decks, tear out walls."

Joel narrowed his eyes on her. "You didn't think to mention that to me? I've been searching for someone to help out over here."

"You never asked."

"I wouldn't think to ask a woman in pink heels if she knew a guy who could erect a wall."

Kennedy moved to the bag of food and pulled out the two containers inside. "You should always ask. It's called networking."

Joel laughed. "Can I meet your brother?"

She shrugged. "As soon as I have words with him over not helping out with my dad today. If he's still speaking to me after that, I'll introduce you to him."

"Fair enough." Joel sat down after Kennedy took a seat. "You look cute in jeans by the way."

"Oh, these old things?" she teased.

"You look like you've wielded a paint brush or two in those."

"Might have."

Joel opened his container and his mouth watered when he saw the ribs and beans. "Did you dress like that so that you could help me paint?"

"I'm prepared to do so if you ask."

"Will you help me paint?"

Kennedy picked up a rib and held it near her mouth. "I will help you paint."

"Will you let me pay you in kisses?"

She bit off a piece of meat and chewed. "I'll let you pay me in kisses."

"Maybe this weekend you'd consider letting me make you breakfast for helping too."

Kennedy lowered the rib back into the container and wiped her hands on a napkin. He wondered if he'd lost her on that one.

"You don't mean me just showing up on Sunday morning to eat breakfast with you, do you?"

Joel moved his chair to be closer to hers. "No, I didn't mean that. However, if that's where you're more comfortable, I'd be okay with it."

"I've known you a month."

"You have. And you've been kissing me for the past three days."

"Kissing doesn't mean I want to have sex with you."

Joel eased back in his seat. "Noted. In fact, the invitation was insensitive of me. You're a classy gal."

"I'm not a prude."

"It's only Wednesday. You have a lot of time to think about it. Let me just say, I make some bad ass omelets." He moved his chair back, picked up a rib and took a bite.

If she didn't want to spend the night with him, he was okay with that. There wasn't any hurry to move things along, even if he was in his mid-thirties, and he felt as if time were fleeting quickly. He wouldn't mention it again. When she was ready to move on from kissing like teenagers, he'd be there.

CHAPTER 21

*D*inner had been discarded, work lights had been turned on, and Joel had cranked up the music. Blake Shelton serenaded them, followed by Hank Williams.

"You're not particular to an era of country music?" Kennedy asked as she loaded up her paint roller and began on the wall with the bank of windows.

"Ya gotta mix in the classics with the new stuff to appreciate it all. Don't be surprised if you get some Patsy Cline, perhaps some old school fiddle, and then it breaks into a Christmas song with the Muppets."

Kennedy snorted out a laugh and looked at him as she loaded up her roller with more paint.

"Muppets?"

"This particular playlist is very eclectic," he informed her as he taped off the door frame to the wall with the patio doors.

"Any Kenny?"

"Rogers?"

"That's the one," she confirmed as she took the paint brush from the top of the can and painted around the light fixture.

Joel pulled his phone from his pocket, slid his finger over the screen, and Kenny Rogers and Linda Ronstadt's *We've Got Tonight* began to play.

The song had always been one of her favorites, as she'd been brought up on Kenny Rogers' music. But tonight the words dug a little deeper after he'd asked her to breakfast.

As she turned to set down the paint brush and pick back up the roller, Joel moved in and took her hand, pulling her toward the center of the room.

With her hand still in his, Joel placed his other hand on the small of her back and began to sway. Instinctively, she rested her other hand on his shoulder.

"Do we really have time to be dancing?" she asked as he pulled her even closer to him.

"Life would suck if you didn't take two minutes to dance once in a while."

Joel pressed his cheek to hers and Kennedy eased against him. His solid frame was comforting. Their hands drew inward, and tucked between their shoulders. Their dance became more of a sway as Kenny and Linda promised each other one night in their song with no need of thinking about tomorrow.

The lyrics pounded in Kennedy's head as Joel's lips came to her neck.

One night, would it be so bad to let go for one night? Could she let go of the proper thought process and stay with him for one night?

Who was she kidding? One night would lead to two. Two nights would make a relationship. Three nights... she had to stop thinking about it, or she would talk herself out of it.

Joel eased back slightly so that his forehead pressed to hers. "Your pulse is really fast."

Her lips trembled as she looked into his dark eyes. "I was just listening to the song."

"This song does that to you?"

She chuckled and licked her lips. "Your invitation did that to me."

He eased back more so that he was fully looking at her now. "My invitation for breakfast?"

Kennedy nodded. "I'm not good at this relationship stuff."

"Says who?"

"Says me. I've never really been in one. Well, not one that I cared about what the other person thought."

"Relationship. The use of the word is a positive. And, even better, my mother adores you."

Kennedy laughed nervously, again. "She's a very dear woman."

"I love my mom."

"And that's part of your endearment."

"Endearment. I'm loving the words you're using," he said as he spun her around and back to him tightly. "Don't take me up on my offer if you're not sure. I'm in no hurry."

Kennedy licked her lips again and stopped moving. "I want to take you up on it."

His eyes lit when she said it. "Are you sure?"

"Not in the least. I might chicken out."

"Noted. There would be no hard feelings. Like you said, I've known you a month and the kissing is new."

"But I rather enjoy the kissing."

Joel moved in and took her mouth, only to make her head swim more. "I do too," he admitted.

Kenny and Linda finished serenading them and the loudest drum beat and screech from a guitar echoed through the empty building as Alex and Eddie Van Halen gave way to David Lee Roth declaring he was hot for his teacher.

Kennedy stepped back and pressed her hands to her ears.

Joel hurried to turn down the speaker as he laughed. "I told you it was an eclectic list."

"I just wasn't prepared for it."

Taking his phone out of his pocket, he changed to another playlist. "This one has no surprises."

Harry Connick Jr. now played, and it instantly soothed Kennedy's nerves. She moved from Joel and went back to painting her wall.

In three days she'd already come to know more about the man than she ever could have imagined when she'd first seen him on that Monday morning outside her store. She'd been intrigued then, though standoffish about it. Now she wondered if she could wait until Saturday. Her insides buzzed and her blood hummed in her veins.

She needed to go to her own home tonight and get a grip on herself. She had a tendency to overthink things, but was always prepared. Sleeping with a man took preparation too.

What would Hillary think of the situation? Kennedy laughed to herself as she loaded the roller with paint. Hillary would be proud, she decided. She wasn't quite as attached to her morals as Kennedy was, and Kennedy had a stranglehold on hers.

It was all going to be okay, and if it didn't work out, well, she could always go to therapy. Lord knows she'd found herself there before, dealing with what her father had done to her mother.

No, she thought again. That was her parents' life, not hers. She wouldn't tolerate being lied to or deceived. If Joel was that kind of man, he'd get kicked to the curb.

She looked over her shoulder and watched his long body stretch out a length of tape on the wall. She'd met his mother. Joel Kingsley wasn't the kind of man who would break her heart on purpose. He was more in jeopardy of getting his heart broken.

CHAPTER 22

*K*ennedy had managed all of Thursday and Friday and most of Saturday without mentioning Joel to Hillary at all. It wasn't until Hillary had seen the sticky note on Kennedy's computer screen with Joel's address, and the message, *can't wait to see you tonight* that the questions began.

She had just finished with a client and was cleaning up the private showroom when Hillary walked in with the note attached to her finger.

"*Can't wait to see you tonight,*" she read the words that had been written at the bottom of the note.

Kennedy narrowed her gaze at her. "Where did you get that?"

"Off your computer. Seriously, if you make me put shipment notices on your desk, I'm going to see these things."

Kennedy swiped the paper from Hillary's finger. "Leave my things alone."

"I don't think I will," she said as she sat down in one of the pink chairs. This thing with you and the guy next door is more serious than I thought. I thought you two were just making out all the time. I didn't know you were sleeping together. Did I miss something?"

Kennedy hung up a jumpsuit that she coveted, but it was in green, and that just wasn't something that would look good on her.

"My relationship with Joel Kingsley is none of your business."

"It kinda is. He's our neighbor, you're my boss. Oh, wait, and my best friend. If you're banging the guy next door after you just met him, I want to know."

"I am not... I'm not doing that." She fumbled for her words. "Besides, I've known him a month. I've met his mother and his brother. It's not like he's some stranger."

"Still, a month is short term for Kennedy Devereaux," Hillary stated, and Kennedy turned.

"Not like you who slept with my brother one time and then moved on."

"Are you judging me or your family? It takes two to tango, and it was a mighty nice tango."

Kennedy cringed. "I don't want any more details. And I'm sorry I was being judgmental."

"I don't worry about that stuff like you do. And for the record, I'm not judging you. You're a successful, grown woman who has the interest of one freaking hot and attentive man. Who wouldn't want to spend the weekend with him?"

Kennedy adjusted the sleeves of a jacket the last client had turned her nose up at, but she knew it would sell within the week.

"I really like him. He's not like any other man I've ever known. He has a sense of family, a work ethic, and he's a damn fine kisser," she said on a breath and felt the heat rise in her cheeks.

"I've seen you kiss him, lots, and I could have told you that." Hillary stood and walked toward the door. "I'm happy for you, Ken. I'm really happy for you."

"Thank you."

"And for what it's worth, your brother..."

Kennedy held up a finger to ward off any more information. "I don't want to hear it."

"You know, there never was a second time with him because of you."

"Don't blame me."

"Oh, I blame you. The hissy fit you threw made it quite clear where you stand with us."

"Neither of you are relationship material. And I don't want to be hurt by either one of you."

Hillary shook her head, but she was still smiling. "It's a good thing we both love you."

"Whatever," Kennedy shook her head as she straightened the outfits on the rack.

"Ken," Hillary said, drawing Kennedy's attention back to the doorway. "He was a really, really, really good kisser." She laughed as she walked away and Kennedy shook off the thought.

The only person holding Kennedy back from enjoying what was going on in her life, was herself. She never wanted to go through the pain her mother went through, and yet, it left her lonely. She looked around the room filled with clothes from Paris and New York. A woman could only be surrounded by pink and beautiful things so much, she decided. At some point she'd need to step outside the box and experience life, or she'd regret it. Perhaps the saying about it being better to have loved and lost was better than not loving at all—or whatever they said—was true. One failed relationship didn't make her horrible at it. Her father's morals were not her own.

Kennedy looked at the time on her phone. She had two more hours at the shop, and then she would go home and put a bag together. She'd hesitated doing so that morning, because she still wasn't sure she wanted to spend the night with Joel, but after talking to Hillary, she was damn sure she wanted to now.

The pile of clothes on her bed was growing, and Kennedy

sorted through nightgowns and pajama bottoms. What the hell was she supposed to pack for a night with a man?

Had she lost sight of all normalcy? He was going to think she was crazy, and yet, she wanted him to think she'd given no thought to it at all.

Would she need a nightgown or a pair of pajamas? After all, this was for sex, right? Or was it? Was she reading it all wrong?

Looking at the mountain of clothes she'd pulled from her closet and dresser, she sat on the floor and reminded herself to breathe. A minute later, she texted her sister to come over and help her pack.

"I don't know what your issue is," Paige said nearly an hour later as she sifted through the clothes. "What do you usually wear on a Saturday night?"

"If I'm cleaning the house, I wear yoga pants and a tank top. If I'm out at the grocery store, a cute pair of boyfriend jeans and a T-shirt. He's used to seeing me in dresses and suits."

"God you're boring," Paige said as she dropped a blouse into the pile. "What were you wearing when he invited you to stay?"

Kennedy winced. "A pair of ratty jeans and a T-shirt. We were painting."

"Perfect. Then go with the boyfriend jeans, that cute T-shirt... this one," she said as she pulled it from a hanger. "Take a comfy pair of shorts and a tank to sleep in if you just can't do the naked in bed thing all night."

Paige sorted through more clothes.

"Take an extra shirt for tomorrow." Paige held up a high necked tank that Kennedy knew showed off her shoulders perfectly. "And this. This is freaking cute on you."

"It is, isn't it."

Paige let out a chuckle. "Don't accessorize like you're going to work. Just a nice, simple chain. Wear your watch, and get the hell out of your house and go."

"This is big."

"It shouldn't be. You act like an old lady, and you're not one. Go have some fun. You deserve it more than anyone I know."

"What if it goes well and I stay an extra day?"

"Then chances are you won't be wearing much of this at all, and you can recycle."

That caused Kennedy to laugh. "I need to lighten up."

"You do. By the way, your house looks great. Did your mom show up and clean?"

That took the humor out of the moment. "No. I did it myself thank you. Okay, you can go now."

"I think I'll wait until you're in your car and I watch you drive away. I still think you're a flight risk."

Kennedy shook her head. Her sister was probably right. She stood, picked up the items her sister had chosen for her, and put them into a leather overnight bag. Every step she took was out of her comfort zone.

CHAPTER 23

*J*oel stood in the doorway and watched as Kennedy pulled into his driveway. She'd actually showed up—he'd had doubts.

She was terrified to spend the evening at his house. He could see it in her eyes when she put her car in park and looked up at him. God, she was adorable.

When she stepped out of the car, he walked down the front steps toward the driveway. Something told him to walk gently, and speak even more gently.

She was dressed in a pair of jeans that were rolled up at the bottom, and a pair of flip-flops exposed *Kennedy Pink* polished toes. She wore a toe ring. And why did that make his belly flip with giddy excitement?

On her wrist was a smartwatch with a fancy band, but none of the other custom pieces she usually wore.

Her hair was in a ponytail, which was then braided. Or did she just have a braid? He didn't know hairstyles, all he knew was she looked casual and cute as hell.

Kennedy pulled a bag from the back seat, and stood there looking at him. "I'm here."

"Thank goodness," he said reaching for her bag. "I thought you had second thoughts."

"I did. I had second, third, and fourth thoughts, too. But Paige and Hillary said I needed to get over myself and come."

"You have very smart friends."

"Paige is my sister."

He nodded slowly. "That's right." Joel moved in and gently kissed her lips. "I have a bottle of wine open and a charcuterie board prepped. There are two steaks seasoned and waiting for a grill, and I stopped and picked up some little tarts from the bakery at the end of your building."

"Wow, I didn't realize you were going to go to this much trouble."

Joel moved his hand to her cheek and held it there as he gazed into her eyes. "I want to impress you, and I think you deserve the best. Next time it might be drive-through from McDonald's."

That made her laugh and he could see her shoulders ease. "I'd be okay with that too. Though I know you just well enough to know you wouldn't put that in your body."

"You have been paying attention. C'mon." Joel took her hand and led her into his house.

Joel opened the screen door and stepped back as she entered his home. Observing her body language, he knew she was taking it all in, just as she had when she'd walked through the door to the tap room.

June Kingsley was a woman who valued a tidy and spotless house, and she passed that down to her two boys. Joel was used to the reaction he got from men and women when they walked into his home.

"You didn't spend the past week cleaning did you?" she asked as she studied the two family photos he had on the wall. One was of the four of them when he was six, and the other was from Jeff's wedding.

"You assumed I had some frat house, bachelor pad?"

"I assume every man has that."

"And I assume you have a plush pink rug in your living room, like the one under your desk. Everything is white, pristine, and completely in order. Your closet is organized by color and style, and all of your purses are situated on shelves and not just thrown in the top of the closet."

Did she just go pale?

Kennedy pushed her shoulders back. "I apologize for the blanket statement. You have a lovely home."

"Thank you," Joel said.

He passed by her and led her to the kitchen, which he, Jeff, and his father had remodeled when he'd moved in years ago. As he set her bag down in the dining room, he watched her look around.

The charcuterie was set up on the island along with two empty glasses and a bottle of red wine.

Kennedy ran her finger down the side of the bottle. "Are you trying to seduce me?"

"Is it working?"

She raised a shoulder and looked out the window to his patio. "Holy cow."

He couldn't help but smile when she moved to the sliding glass door and pulled it open. Following her out to the deck, he let her soak in the oasis he'd built for himself.

"Is that a koi pond?"

Joel moved in next to her and rested his hand at the small of her back. "Yes. My sister-in-law gave them to me as a joke, I think. She wondered if I could care for anything long enough to keep them alive."

Kennedy turned her head to look at him. "And what was the verdict?"

"The pond has been well maintained for nearly three years now. I'm not sure what point she was trying to make, but I take care of what's mine."

The string of lights that illuminated the patio overhead clicked on as the sun crept toward the horizon. Kennedy looked up and smiled at them before turning into his arms.

"You have a beautiful home," she said as she laced her arms around his neck, and he pulled her closer.

"Thank you. The tap room will be amazing soon too."

"Of course it will. I painted one of the walls," she teased as she leaned in and initiated the first kiss of the night.

As her soft, warm lips parted to his, he thought that she belonged in the beautiful surroundings of his home. She was the piece of art that had been missing. No one who had ever been there, or lived there, quite compared to Kennedy Devereaux.

Her fingers tangled in his hair, and he reacted by splaying his hands down over her tight, curved bottom. A moan escaped her throat as he did so, but she didn't pull back. Instead, she leaned into him more.

His home was beautiful because he appreciated beautiful things, not to seduce women. But it seemed to have worked on Kennedy, whom he thought was the most beautiful thing God could have created.

A month ago, he never could have imagined that he'd have the woman, draped in pink with the judgmental stare, in his arms. Thank goodness his mother taught him to look past a person's exterior and find what lies beneath.

CHAPTER 24

*K*ennedy decided that she could live on Joel's patio forever. The house was twice as nice, but the patio, the roses, the twinkling lights, they appealed to her.

They'd carried the charcuterie board out to the patio and drank wine once they decided that they'd each gone light-headed from the kiss they'd enveloped themselves in.

She sat and watched Joel work the grill. Steaks on one side, potatoes wrapped in foil on the other side, and a plate of asparagus waited for its moment on the grill. Her cooking skills were limited to opening a package and putting it into the microwave.

Kennedy thought she should feel intimidated, but she didn't. Joel had a different set of skills than she did, and she appreciated that.

Kennedy sipped her wine as he pulled the steaks from the grill and set them on a plate, and then tented them with tin foil. Turning, he winked at her as he set the plate on the table and then put the asparagus on the grill.

"Where did you learn to do all of that?" she asked.

He turned, picked up his glass of wine, and sipped. "What? Grill?"

She nodded. "I'm a master with the microwave."

Setting his glass back down, he gave the asparagus a turn by rolling his tongs over them. "My dad grilled a lot while I was growing up, but so did my mom." He cocked his head to the side. "So did both of my grandfathers, my uncles, and the next door neighbor. Though, he did set his house on fire trying to barbecue in the garage."

Kennedy hid her laugh behind her glass as she sipped her wine. "Was he hurt?"

"Lost his eyebrows and his Harley. But, the house was saved by the brave volunteer fire department, headed by my dad."

He was a freaking page out of a story book, Kennedy decided. What was it like to admire your family so much you included uncles and grandfathers in your stories?

She swallowed hard, trying not to let her own story interfere in her happiness of the moment. Maybe with this man, she could create that kind of story.

The very thought scared the hell out of her, and as she took the next sip of wine, she choked and spilled it down the front of her, staining the white shirt she'd painstakingly picked out with Paige's help.

Joel's eyes went wide as he hurried to her. "Are you okay?"

"Shit!" Kennedy stood up, the wine glass still in her hand.

"I've worked with wine before. I have club soda. We'll soak it in the sink. You're welcome to one of my T-shirts. I have to stay with the grill. Go in the house, down the hall, second door on the right. Pick anything in the closet." He pressed a solid kiss to her lips. "Go, this will be done when you get back."

Kennedy handed him the glass, which he set down on the table, and hurried inside his house. One thing was tried and true when it came to Kennedy and relationships, she could always muck it up somehow.

She walked down the hallway, just as he'd told her to, but she walked slowly looking at the rows of photos that lined the hallway. Vacations—the four of them. Graduations—the four of them. Weddings—the four of them. She swallowed hard feeling the sting of tears clogging her throat. Did she have a photo of her and her siblings all together? She knew, for a fact, that she had only two of them with her, her mother, her father, and Max. They weren't the typical family—well how could they be when Chase came between them and belonged to another woman?

Kennedy came to the door, second on the right, and she walked into the bedroom where Joel slept. She was met by a king-sized four post bed with matching dresser, mirror, and bedside tables. Blinds were tilted, letting in the evening light and shadowing the dark gray walls. There was a lamp in the corner next to a plush chair with ottoman and a book which rested on the seat of the chair.

Batting her eyes against the sting of tears that still threatened, she looked at the book. Stephen Hawking—God, he didn't even read lightly.

There was a master bathroom, and just like the kitchen—and the rest of the house—it was beautifully remodeled in grays and glass.

Across the room was a closet with mirrored doors. She slid them to the side to expose the fastidious workman's collection of T-shirts and jeans. Chuckling, she reached for a T-shirt with the Route 66 emblem on it. Because she couldn't help herself, she stood and admired the clothes, separated by color and kind. There were T-shirts, polos, and button down shirts. A small rack of ties, and on the floor, three pairs of sneakers, cowboy boots, flip-flops, and a brand-new pair of work boots, no doubt waiting for their chance to be worn. His jeans were categorized by how worn they were, and that made her chuckle.

Obviously, there were work jeans in various shades of worn out, and dark denim that was probably saved for nice outings and were paired with the cowboy boots. There was one suit, and she had to assume that was saved for weddings and funerals. Her father owned one suit, and that was when he would wear it.

"Did you find one?" she heard Joel ask from the door where he leaned against the doorjamb.

"I did. Sorry, I was admiring your closet."

"My brother says I have a problem."

"A problem? How is this a problem?"

He moved to stand next to her and look into his closet. "I like things a certain way. And most people don't look at a man in worn work boots, unshaven face, and paint stains on their shirt and think this is where they choose clothes from each morning."

"You're right, but there's nothing wrong with it."

He smiled and pulled her to him. "Good, then my freaky ways don't bother you." He nipped her lips with a kiss. "I can't wait to see your closet."

"You'll be sorely disappointed," she said stepping back. "I'm going to change into this, in your bathroom," she added. "I'll be out in a moment."

He kissed her again. "I filled the sink in the laundry room with club soda. You can soak your shirt in there. It's just off the kitchen."

She nodded and watched as he walked out of the room.

Slowly, she let out a long breath. She was in love with the man —no doubt—it was love.

CHAPTER 25

*S*ometimes Joel surprised even himself with his grilling skills. He'd burnt many steaks in his time, but the ones he'd made for dinner this evening had to be some of his best.

Or maybe it was the woman seated across from him in his Route 66 T-shirt that made dinner taste so much better.

She'd eased once the stain came out of her shirt, and he'd kissed her senseless one more time. Now she sat sipping wine, her legs casually crossed, and her bare foot bouncing to the beat of the music on the speaker. This was a scene he'd created in his head a million times, he thought. The perfect woman, the perfect setting, and an exceptional sunset. She'd taken a few bites of the tart from the bakery, but hadn't devoured it like he had his. Maybe she'd consider sharing if she wasn't into sweets. Usually he'd stop himself, but he'd add an extra set of reps in the basement gym tomorrow to make up for it. Well, that was if he wanted to. If Kennedy stayed all day, that would be a bonus he would take.

"Aren't you going to finish your tart?" he asked, and she lazily shifted her gaze toward him.

"I'm so full that I think I might explode."

Joel laughed as Michael Bublé began to serenade them. He stood, offered Kennedy his hand, and pulled her to her feet. Wrapping his arm around her, he swayed from side to side as she put her hand on his chest. He'd never tire of dancing with her.

"I'm so glad you came here tonight," he whispered.

"So am I."

As they swayed, he pressed his lips to her neck, and he felt her breath against his cheek. The sway slowed as he pressed kisses from her earlobe to her collarbone.

Kennedy planted her hands on his shoulder and eased him back. "Take me inside," she pleaded on a heavy breath. "to your bedroom."

The moment called for it, he thought as he scooped her legs up into his arms and her arms came around his neck. He carried her over the threshold and down the hall while she pressed kisses to his neck.

Laying her on his bed, he looked down at her. He wanted to remember every moment. In his heart he knew this was the last first time. Why it crossed his mind, he wasn't sure. There was just something about Kennedy Devereaux that made him never want to have anything to do with another woman again.

Propping up on her elbows, she looked up at him with dark eyes. "Are you having second thoughts?" she asked and all he could do was smiled down at her.

"I'm appreciating every moment, that's all."

A smile formed on her lips, and she sat up on the bed. Taking the hem of the T-shirt he'd worn so many times, she lifted it up and over her head. Now she sat on his bed in only her jeans and a pink bra, and he wondered if it too had a custom color. If it wasn't custom, it should carry her name too. *Kennedy Pink* accented her skin and made her even more appealing.

The smile on her lips widened as she reached for the front clasp on her bra and opened it.

The air in his lungs stuck. He found it harder to breathe

looking at the woman laying before him. She was lovely, and that wasn't the word he usually used when he was in such a situation.

"Are you going to join me?" she asked as she inched up further onto the bed.

Joel wasn't sure his feet would take him the few inches toward her. Pulling his own shirt over his head, he watched as Kennedy eased up on her elbows.

"Wow," she said. "You really don't put any crap in your body, do you?"

He eased a hand over his abdomen before lowering himself down next to her. "You get one body."

"And yours is perfect," she said as she pressed her hand to his bare chest.

"Might I say, ditto?"

She laughed casually as she moved her hand from his chest and up into his hair.

"I want to see the rest." She pulled him to her and kissed him, pressing her breasts to his bare skin. The rest was autopilot, because his mind had disconnected from his body. His body registered the pleasure of her body, her touch, her kisses—but his mind was stuck in the thought that this woman was his one and only.

The moments had turned into hours, and there was a peacefulness at two in the morning where Kennedy found herself completely drained of energy and devoid of the usual thoughts that plagued her mind. Wrapped in Joel's arms, her cheek pressed to his bare chest and his heart thumping against her cheek, she was truly at peace.

She'd never wanted to spend the whole day in bed wrapped in a man's arms. Her mind would never let her. There were too many things to do in her life, this was usually a luxury she wouldn't give herself. But not today, she thought. Not with him. This was perfect, and she would let herself worry about that later, because it would worry her. That morning when he was standing in front of her shop looking in the window, this was the furthest thought from her mind. How had they ended up here?

Joel ran his hand down the back of her matted hair and pressed a kiss to the top of her head. "I think I am officially worn out," he chuckled as he squeezed her closer to him. "This is a dinner date that will go down in the books."

The words worried her for a moment. Men didn't think like women, and she needed to remember that. She usually didn't think like most women, but she was finding herself too comfortable with him, and her mind had more than once drifted to how temporary this situation was. How many more women would come through his tap room and end up where she was?

Kennedy squeezed her eyes closed tightly. No, she wasn't going to let that thought take over the pleasantness of the night. In that very moment, she was Joel's, and he was hers. That was how she wanted to remember it. That was what she wanted.

CHAPTER 26

*I*t was nearly eight-thirty in the morning when Joel managed to put his feet on the ground and walk toward the bathroom. Kennedy breathed deeply in the bed, and he was going to let her stay right there.

He pulled on a pair of shorts, ran his fingers through the mess of hair on top of his head, and decided to brush his teeth. Leaving her to rest, he walked to the kitchen and started a pot of coffee. Joel turned on the TV and tuned it to ESPN to get the updates from games he might have missed the night before. The dishes from last night waited for him, and he loaded them into the dishwasher. Normally, he'd have left the kitchen tidy, but they were in a bit of a hurry once dinner had been finished.

After pouring himself a cup of coffee, he turned off the TV and went out to the back porch to sit. Usually, even on Sundays, he'd be poring over details about the tap house, or would have already been on site, but he'd warned his brother that he was taking the day off, and he'd even turned off his phone. He was fairly sure he'd seen Kennedy do the same.

"You didn't wake me."

Her voice still dripped with sleep, and when he turned to see her standing in the doorway, his heart did a little flip.

She was in the T-shirt she'd borrowed the night before and her panties. Her blonde hair had been piled atop her head in a makeshift bun with a pencil stuck through it. Leaning up against the door frame, she crossed her ankles, accentuating the long muscles of her legs. She blew into the mug of coffee she held between her hands. There had never—ever—been a more beautiful sight.

"Did you sleep well?" he asked, watching her take in the beauty of his back yard.

"I did. Are those hummingbird feeders?" She nodded toward the back corner of the yard.

Joel nodded. "My mother's idea. She put them there."

She didn't move toward him, but smiled when he mentioned his mother. "You're all very close, aren't you?"

"Too close sometimes."

"I don't think there's such a thing. I saw how you and your brother ran to my store when you saw her there. It's very sweet."

"You're close to your mother too, aren't you?"

Kennedy shrugged a shoulder toward her ear. "Yes. We are very close, but she always holds a little grudge because Max and I are close to Paige and Chase too. She desperately wants to hate that, but appreciates our closeness. However, it puts a little bite into nearly every conversation."

"She never remarried?"

Her eyes widened. "Oh, she's remarried. I didn't mention that the other night, huh?"

He shook his head.

Kennedy walked toward him, setting her coffee on the small table, and then landed in his lap. Yes, he could get used to this.

"She's been married to Ted since I was about eight. He's a good man. He takes good care of my mom, doesn't have any kids of his own, so Max and I were his world too."

It was funny to him that she hadn't mentioned Ted in her original story.

"What should we do today?" he thought it was safer to change the subject.

Kennedy pressed a kiss to his neck. "Do we have to do anything productive?"

"Not at all. I think we will both go crazy, but no, we don't have to be productive."

"You're right. About one o'clock I'll be stir crazy."

"What do you usually do on Sundays?"

"I go into the store and clean. It doesn't take long. We clean all week. There's no reason that the bathroom can't be cleaned when I get there tomorrow."

Joel laid a gentle kiss just above her breast. "It'll ruin your Monday morning manicure."

"You have been paying attention, haven't you?"

"You have no idea."

Joel stood, scooping Kennedy up in his arms. "Let's take an hour to think about the rest of the day," he offered taking her mouth as he walked through the door.

"An hour? Aren't you exhausted?"

"Very."

"But you have energy for this?"

"Oh, something tells me that I'll always have energy to do this with you."

An hour later they showered and decided on a very late breakfast. As Kennedy braided her hair, Joel pulled together the items for a brunch.

He watched as Kennedy set her overnight bag by the front door, and it saddened him that their time would end, and she'd go home. But what more could he expect? He'd asked her for one night, and he got one night.

"I don't have real bacon, just turkey," he said as he watched her pull her phone from her purse and turn it on. Obviously, she needed to connect with the rest of the world.

"I'm fine with that," she said as her brows drew together.

"Do you like orange juice? Freshly squeezed yesterday."

"Um, sure," she muttered as she scrolled through her phone and then it rang in her hand.

"Paige, what's going on?" She nodded, her eyes wide.

Joel removed the pan from the stove and walked toward the doorway.

"Paige, you knew where I was. Yes, I did turn off my phone, but..." Her cheeks had gone red. "Where is he? Why didn't they just take him somewhere closer? Don't yell at me." Kennedy moved the phone and looked down at the screen. "Max is calling me now. I'll be there. Paige, I'll talk to you later."

He watched as she ended one call and connected another.

"I heard. I'll be there. Where are you?" She shook her head. "I said I'd be there and where I am right now is none of your damn business. Fine."

She disconnected the call.

"Something's wrong?" Joel moved toward her, but kept some space.

"My dad had some episode on the cruise ship. I don't know if it was a heart attack or what. No one has a full answer, they're just mad at me because I need to make some decisions as if they are all incapable."

"Okay," he said gently as he touched her arm. "Everyone is probably a little worried. So where are they taking your dad?"

When she lifted her eyes to meet his they were filled with tears. "He's being brought by helicopter to St. Paul's."

"Here in town?"

"Yes."

"How long?"

The first tear fell. "I don't know. Paige said an hour."

"Then we can be there when he gets there. I'm going to make

us each a little something to eat on the way. You didn't hear from Chase yet?"

"They said he wouldn't answer, so that probably means he's asleep."

"Do you want to stop by his place?"

Kennedy nodded.

Joel laid a gentle kiss on her cheek. "Okay, give me five minutes, and we'll be on our way."

CHAPTER 27

*T*here was a new side to Kennedy Devereaux that Joel was witnessing, he decided. This Kennedy was vulnerable, scared, and she wept.

As she directed Joel to Chase's place, Max would keep her updated via text and Paige would call, hang up, and call again. It seemed a bit manic, but then again, he had no idea how he would handle a similar situation. The childish side of him always thought that emergencies were handled like the Transformers where they would call for the Autobots to assemble. Everyone picked up what they were doing and headed out.

The very thought had him snicker to himself, and luckily Kennedy was too engaged in a conversation with Paige to have noticed.

"His house is up on the left."

"Got it," he said, noticing the three limousines that were parked next to the house. "He doesn't have a location where he keeps the cars?"

She looked at him, narrowed her eyes, and then opened them wide again. "Oh, no. This keeps his costs down. However, the neighbors have told him if he gets one more they'll take action against him."

"So he's looking for a place to keep them?"

She shook her head. "No, it means he's looking for one more car."

And that, he assumed, wrapped up the personality of Chase Devereaux, the way his sister saw him.

The moment Joel pulled up in front of the house, Kennedy jumped from his truck and headed to the front door. She lifted the corner of the mat on the step and pulled the hidden key from underneath it.

Without even knocking first, she unlocked the door, and pushed it in.

Kennedy hated Chase's house. Though hers had needed a thorough cleaning, Chase's was a full on bachelor pad, and had the musty smell to go along with it.

Jasper, his elderly hound dog, lifted his head when he saw her. She took a moment, waiting for him to bark or come after her as a guard dog should. Instead, Jasper lowered his head and went back to sleep.

With a shake of her head, she called out to her brother. "Chase! Chase! Where the hell are you?"

She turned down the hall toward his bedroom and saw more than two legs emerging from under the sheets.

Crap!

"Chase!" she yelled one more time.

Her brother's head popped off the pillow, his blond hair matted, and the stunned brunette next to him screamed.

The brunette must have decided Kennedy wasn't a threat when Chase sat up calmly and wiped his eyes.

"Just let your damn self into my damn house," he said as he tried to focus on her.

"This place stinks."

"You're not my mom."

"She'd be disappointed, I'm sure. We have to go."

The brunette covered herself up with the sheet and tucked herself in behind Chase as if for shelter.

"I don't remember us having plans."

"Damnit! Get up. They're flying dad to the hospital from the cruise ship. He's had a heart attack or something."

Chase's eyes went wide, and he put his feet on the floor as if to stand. Looking around he realized the brunette had gathered the sheet, so he reached for his pants on the floor, then exchanged glances with Kennedy.

"Would you mind turning around?"

Letting out a ragged breath, Kennedy turned and listened as Chase stepped into his jeans.

"Stay as long as you like. Let yourself out the side door. It'll lock on its own," he said to the woman laying on the bed as he passed Kennedy pulling on a T-shirt.

She followed him to the front door. "You're just leaving her here?"

"I don't own anything I'd care about being stolen."

"Who is she?" Kennedy asked as Chase grabbed his boots as they walked through the door and closed it behind them.

"Can't remember her name. Bridesmaid for the wedding I'm driving next week."

"And you met her early when she came to inspect the limo?"

He chuckled. "I met her when she came back to the car during the bachelorette party, and we had our own party."

Kennedy let out a disgusted sigh and then nearly plowed into the back of Chase as he abruptly stopped.

"Hmmm, what's this? Isn't he the guy from the bar next to your shop?" he asked with a slight tone of humor.

"Joel. You met him."

"I sure did. One time. And on a Sunday morning, you have on

casual clothes and your hair pulled back. Is he going to help you clean your store, or were you rudely interrupted too?"

"It's none of your business."

"Though it was yours to ask who the woman was in my bed?"

Kennedy set her jaw. "At least I know his name, have met his mother and his brother, and been seen in public with him on numerous occasions."

The corner of her brother's mouth turned up into a smile. "Has he met your mother yet?"

"No."

"Interesting. So how is he? Was this your first weekender? Wait, let me calculate. You've known him a month, so you have a good, oh, six months before you..."

Kennedy held up a finger to stop his rant. "Are you driving with us or taking your own car?"

"I'll go with you."

As she started for Joel's truck, Chase reached for her arm and stopped her.

"Dad, is he okay?"

So, she thought, he had been paying attention. "I don't know. We don't know too much."

He pulled her in and wrapped his arms around her. She wriggled enough to not have her nose pressed to his stale shirt.

"He's going to be okay, Ken. He's much too stubborn to let anything really happen to him. This will be one of his great adventures."

Kennedy eased against her brother. Deep down, she knew he was right. Her father did like to shake things up, and wouldn't he be loving the fact that all four of his children would be at the hospital waiting for him when he got there?

*a*s Joel parked the truck in the parking lot of the hospital, Chase pointed out Max's truck as he parked further down the aisle.

"See, Max is not rushing either," he said and Kennedy shook her head.

"Maybe he knows something we don't know. They're flying Dad in."

"Right. We're all going to be sitting here for hours before he gets here."

Kennedy turned around in her seat to look at her brother and offer him a piece of gum. "You're a jerk."

Chase shrugged, took the gum, and popped the piece in his mouth.

Kennedy stepped out of the truck and waved down Max, as Chase and Joel stepped out too.

"Is he here?" she asked and Max surveyed the three of them quizzically.

"About twenty to forty minutes out. Paige is inside on the cardiac floor where they're going to put him and run tests. Some woman he met on the cruise is flying in with them. And what the hell were you doing last night?" He directed the question to Chase. "You look and smell like shit."

"This is what you get when your sister literally pulls you out of bed when there is still company in it."

Kennedy bit down on her lip to stifle the comments that wanted to fly from her mouth. Instead, she turned to Joel. "Joel, this is our brother Max."

Joel stepped forward, hand extended. "Joel Kingsley."

"Max Devereaux." Max shook his hand. "You got dragged into this how?"

Kennedy managed her body between the two men. "Joel is my friend and neighbor at the store. He gave us a ride."

She noticed Joel taking a step back after she said that. It had sounded curt and dismissive, but she wasn't going to get into what she'd been doing with Joel. What she wanted to do was find Paige and get some answers.

As they turned to head toward the building, Joel took her arm and slowed her progression to follow her brothers.

"Why don't I leave you to this. You have plenty of support right now, and I'll just be in the way," he said, and she knew she'd wounded him with what she'd said.

"What if I need you?"

"Then I'm a phone call away. The four of you need some time together. Right now you don't need your friends in the way."

Kennedy dropped her shoulders. "I'm sorry about that. I didn't know what to tell him."

Joel rubbed a hand down her arm. "I know. I suppose we'll have to talk about that. Just so you know, I'm all in. When you have some time, decide where you're comfortable and let me know. But for now, go. Your sister is waiting, and since your brothers are standing at the door waiting. I'm guessing they need your leadership through this."

Kennedy looked toward the door. "I'll call you."

Joel leaned in and kissed her cheek. "I'll answer."

He walked back to the truck, and Kennedy could only stand there, as if frozen in place as she watched him back out and drive away.

He was all in.

Was she?

Paige was in the waiting room and stood from her chair when the elevator opened and the three of them stepped off.

"You found them." The comment was directed at Max.

"In the parking lot. They came together, though Chase looks like shit."

Chase raked his fingers through the blond mess atop his head. "You know, asshole, not all of us have a regal look to us. And some of us were lucky enough to be in bed with a woman when their sister yanked them out of the room."

Max, in his dark denim jeans, pressed T-shirt, and wavy dark —precisely cut hair—moved toward his brother. "What was her name?"

"Go to hell."

"Seriously, bro. What was her name?"

"Does it even matter?"

"It should. You have no respect. You're a pig."

"You're a wussy."

"I beg your pardon?"

"You would."

The men were now chest to chest and Paige and Kennedy moved in to separate them.

Paige thumped them both on the chest. "Stop it. Dad doesn't need this right now. So Chase is loose with morals. Max is so tight with them, he probably has a diamond up his ass, and yes, Kennedy is sleeping with her business neighbor."

All heads turned her direction, and she felt her jaw drop. "Thanks for that."

"Let's just get it all out there so we can stop this nonsense."

Paige pulled them all toward the corner of the room and made them sit. "He's almost here. Initial findings are it wasn't necessarily a heart attack, but he has some blockage. They're going to assess him when he gets here, and he will more than likely have surgery."

Kennedy's hand came to her lips and Max wrapped an arm around her shoulder.

Paige straightened her back. "He needs all of us right now, and I don't want the three of you pulling some *he wasn't there for me* crap. We need to support him through this." Paige put her hand out between the four of them as if she were running a sports team. Chase laid his atop Paige's, then Max, and finally Kennedy. "We're in this together. We're a team. And no matter who is sleeping with whom," she raised her brows, "we support each other. Devereauxs don't give up on one another."

Instead of pumping their hands up and down and shouting *Go Team!* they grabbed hold of one another's hands and each took a breath.

Paige was right. Devereauxs never gave up on one another, even if they fought. They were a team, and they were there for their father.

Only now, Kennedy wished Joel was there for her.

CHAPTER 29

*B*efore Joel could even put his truck in park, his mother was standing on the front porch. She folded a kitchen towel in her hands, opened it up, and folded it again as he walked toward her.

"A Sunday morning visit from my son? To what do I owe the honor?" she teased as he reached her.

Kissing his mother on the cheek, he looked at her. Sixty years old, and she could pass for his sister, he thought. "I just needed to get out of the house and could use some company."

She nodded, but he knew she read through it all. "C'mon in. Coffee is hot. Dad is just finishing up in the back yard. He got a new mower."

Joel laughed. "He got a new mower two years ago."

"Yes, he did. He likes his new toys."

"And you?"

She only smiled. "He deserves to have what he wants. He's always worked so hard."

And that was one of the things Joel loved about his mother. She appreciated the work his father had always put into to his business and his family. There never had to be justification when any of them wanted something, whether it was material or physically something they wanted to do. When he and Jeff quit their jobs to open the first tap house, and they had to take out a sizable loan, there was no lecture from either of their parents—only support. In time, Joel hoped that he could be a parent like his own. They were loyal to one another and loyal to their children and their friends. He thought he and Jeff had followed in their footsteps thus far.

As he passed by his mother and into her pristine and organized house, he thought about Kennedy and the story of her father. What was it like to grow up not trusting the very people who gave you life? Did she always second guess the motives of everyone, solely based on her father doing what he did?

Joel heard the sound of the mower and then it silenced as his mom walked back to the kitchen. His father looked toward the house, as if he knew he was watching from the window. Joel waved and his father held out his hands to draw attention to the new mower. Joel gave his father a thumbs up as the mower roared back to life.

"I told him to buy a riding mower next," his mother said as she pulled two coffee mugs from the cupboard and filled them.

"Why would he want that?"

"I would think he'd want that because his knee is bad. But he says that it will just make him old to have to ride around on a lawn mower. This one keeps him young."

"I guess he knows what he's talking about."

His mother set a mug in front of him, kissed the top of his head, and then sat down across from him. "What's worrying your head?" she asked as she sipped her coffee, watching him from over the top of her mug.

What did he want to tell her? He'd come to her, so he'd have to tell her something. But wasn't that the problem? He didn't know what to tell her.

"I'm seeing Kennedy Devereaux."

The smile on his mother's lips said she approved. "She is a delightful woman."

"She is."

"She's smart and beautiful. She's got an amazing business sense, and knows what her customers want."

Joel laughed. "I already said I was seeing her. You don't have to sell her."

"I just want you to know what I see in her." She set her mug down. "However, I assume something about this new relationships is bothering you and that's why you're here."

And that was why he always ended up at June Kingsley's kitchen table. She could read him, and it got him talking.

"Her family dynamics are a little different from ours and it seems to hinder our moving forward, though I'm projecting that because this is new."

"What makes you think its hindering your relationship?"

"Because she spent the night last night, and then introduced me to her brothers as her friend."

His mother sipped her coffee. "Where is she now?"

"At the hospital with her family. Her father had a heart attack or something."

Now his mother's eyes had grown wide, and she set the mug down. "And you're here with me?"

"I feel as though I was dismissed, but really, I chose to leave."

"What happened to him?"

Joel spun his mug on the table until he noticed his mother watching with the anticipation that he would spill the coffee, then he stopped. "He was on a cruise and had a heart attack, they think. They were flying him back home."

"That's horrible. I'm sure she's distraught."

"I don't know how to read the situation. She has her brothers and her sister there, but it seems as if they need her to make the big decisions. Or maybe she just assumes that's the situation and it adds more stress to her."

"So why are you here then? Just to tell me you're in love with the girl next door?"

There was a tightening in his chest. "I don't think I said I was in love with her. I said I was seeing her."

"Joel Kingsley, I've only heard you talk about one other person like this, and we know you didn't feel about her like you feel about Kennedy. You don't have to tell me you love her. I'm your mother. I just know."

Joel reached across the table and took his mother's hand in his. "You're right. I do think I'm in love with her. I think it's much too soon to feel that way or to tell her that."

"When you know it, you just know it." She gave Joel's hand a squeeze. "Why don't you go to the hospital and check on her. Just see if she or her siblings need anything. A goodwill gesture, if you will. You're smart enough to read the situation from there."

"The moment I left her, I drove straight here. I guess it was as if my heart and my truck knew what I needed."

"I appreciate that you still need your mother. Now hurry to her before your dad comes back in and wants to have a beer with you."

Joel stood, kissed his mother on the cheek, and headed back to Kennedy.

CHAPTER 30

The coffee in the paper cup in Kennedy's hand sloshed because she shook. It was her fourth cup while her father had been prepped and finally wheeled into surgery. Still, she couldn't decide why they hadn't taken him to a closer hospital. The comfort in him being near home told her it wasn't such a big deal—right? He was going to be okay.

The four of them, Kennedy and her siblings, sat huddled in the corner of the waiting room while Gloria, the woman who came in the helicopter with him, sat alone near the door. She, too, was on her fourth cup of coffee.

Max nudged Kennedy's knee. "You should go talk to her."

Kennedy narrowed her eyes on him. "Me? Why me? You go talk to her."

Max eased back in his chair. "Yeah, right. Not my style."

The man was a piece of work, she thought, handing her brother her coffee. He was a good-looking business man. Seriously, how was it he couldn't start a conversation even if his life depended on it? Paige and Chase had managed some kind of position where they were propped up, back to back, and both asleep in the chairs.

Kennedy stood to make her way to Gloria, and as she did, she managed to bump into her sleeping siblings enough to stir them. There was some satisfaction in that.

Gloria looked up at her as she neared, and smiled. Kennedy felt compelled to do the same as she sat across from the woman who also looked as if she'd been up all night.

"Kennedy, right?" Gloria asked.

"Yes."

"Carl spoke highly of you. Well, of all of you." Her voice shook and so did her hand as she lifted the paper cup to her lips and sipped. "I know he was comforted by you all being here. It was his choice to fly back home instead of going to a local hospital."

And that answered that. But Kennedy now wondered just how much that was going to cost.

"Can I get you anything?" Kennedy asked, not knowing what more to say to the woman, because the firing of questions that she had in mind would probably make the woman cry.

"Your company is enough," Gloria smiled again, sipped her coffee, winced, and set it on the table to her side. "I'm sure you're all wondering who the hell I am."

"There is some curiosity."

"Carl and I met on the cruise and hit it off before we ever left the dock. He's a wonderful man, your father."

Kennedy nodded. "Yeah, he's a good one." She was sure each of his kids could fill her in on how loose he was with his heart. Had he told her exactly how his love life to that point had gone? Marriage, infidelity, loss? "It does seem a bit extreme that you flew here with him. You're missing the end of your cruise and, I'm sorry, where do you live?"

She smiled sweetly. "Miami. But I have friends that will watch my place for now. I'm a snowbird. I live in Miami during the winter and Minnesota during the summer. This year, I opted for a vacation, so I didn't go back to Minnesota. My kids were supportive. I didn't let them know I was here. I'll give that a few days. They won't be looking for word from me for another three days."

And Kennedy thought that made Gloria just a little nervous— the telling her kids that she'd flown off with some guy who had a heart attack.

"How many children do you have?"

Gloria's eyes lit up at the question. "Two. My son and his wife have two children, and those babes are my entire world. I should spend more time with them, but I do enjoy my lifestyle," she added. "My daughter, I'd peg you to be her same age, she's a teacher. She recently divorced, and it's very sad. She had wanted babies, and, well..." Gloria picked up the coffee again, as if she'd forgotten the face she'd made earlier, she took another sip.

"I can get you a fresh one," Kennedy offered.

Gloria set the cup down again. "I should get some water and take a walk. Thank you for taking a moment with me. I promise I'll take good care of your father."

Gloria stood and walked out of the room and Kennedy watched, wide-eyed, as she left. Max fell into the chair next to her the moment Gloria was out of sight.

"What's the look for?" he asked.

"She promised she'd take good care of Dad. What the hell does that mean? He found some woman on a cruise and now she's moving in to take care of him. What the actual hell?"

Max crossed his arms over his chest and furrowed his brow. "We'll talk to him. That doesn't work for us. We'll take care of him."

Kennedy turned to him. "Oh, yeah. When do any of us have time? We all own our own businesses and have our own lives too. What you mean is I'll take care of him."

"You don't have to turn your bitch on for me, Ken. I know you're one."

Kennedy swiftly slapped Max's arm hard enough he winced. "Don't push me, Maxwell."

"We'll get it taken care of," Max said as he rubbed his arm. "No one asked you to be the cruise director, as it were. So chill the hell out. The doctor said this surgery was simple. He'll be in and out. There isn't going to be any babysitting Dad."

Kennedy felt her bottom lip quiver and the tears began to well in her eyes. "Maybe we should babysit him. He obviously can't be left to his own devices. He's proven that since the before I was born."

Max put his arm around her shoulders. "So he's not the perfect man. He's proven that over and over. But you can't say he hasn't been a great dad. He's put in the time to take care of all of us, and the circumstances weren't awesome. We will all be here for him. And, aside from all of us, he's all Paige has, so we have to think of that."

That was a blow that landed right in Kennedy's chest. Their dad was all Paige had, Max was right. It would be devastating to lose both parents before thirty.

"Maybe I should go for a walk. Clear my head," Kennedy said wiping away her tears. "I'll be back in a few minutes."

Max gave her one last squeeze before she stood and headed toward the elevators.

CHAPTER 31

*J*oel walked toward the main doors of the hospital, and when they opened, Kennedy walked out of them.

She stood for a moment watching him walk toward her. He smiled, and wondered if that was insensitive, but he couldn't help it. Seeing her brought joy to his heart, and he'd been looking for that missing element in his life for years.

The moment Joel reached her, she fell into his arms and sobbed against his chest.

"Whoa, hey." He pressed a kiss to the top of her head and attempted to soothe her by running his hand down her back. "What happened? Your dad?"

Kennedy sniffed and shifted so she now stood in front of him wiping her eyes. "I guess I just needed to let it out. I'm so sorry."

Joel caressed her shoulder. "Never be sorry for being human. And never be sorry for using my chest to cry on. It's yours to do so whenever you need. But really, what happened?"

Kennedy took his hand and led him to a bench near the entrance. She sat down, and he followed suit. She rested their interlaced fingers on her thigh and studied them.

"I'm just overwhelmed. Dad's in surgery. Chase is asleep in the waiting room, and so is Paige, though she's worked up, and she should be. He's her only parent." Kennedy let out a hard breath. "Max is keeping his cool as he does, and Gloria, the woman my dad met on the ship and who flew home with him, she's nice enough, I guess. Honestly, I just think I should be handling it better."

"You can't always be in charge. Some things you have to sit the sidelines and wait for," he offered his wisdom, but then second guessed it when she turned her head and narrowed her eyes at him.

"Do you think I'm bossy?"

"I think you're organized and think things through."

"I'm not organized."

"Okay."

"Would that change your perception of me?"

Joel ran his tongue over his teeth. Was she picking a fight? Maybe, but he would steer clear of it. She was vulnerable right now, and he'd learned to steer clear from these kinds of fights through experience. He wasn't going to let Kennedy push him away.

"My perception of you isn't based on your organization skills or the color on the front door of your store. It's based on how I feel when you're around me. I happen to like the disheveled version of Kennedy Devereaux as much as I like the prim and proper version." He brushed a loose piece of hair back behind her ear. "What I see is an older sister that worries about her family—a family that depends on her wisdom. And I see a scared little girl who can't fix her father by herself. Organized or not, I like who you are, Kennedy. I look forward to many more opportunities to get to know you."

She blinked the tears from her eyes and a smile slowly formed on her lips. "You're not going to let me push you away, are you?"

"Are you trying to?"

She chuckled. "Not on purpose. Where did you go when you left? When I was being bitchy."

At least she'd owned up to it, he thought, even though he'd never call her out on it. "I went to my parents' house and had a nice talk with my mother."

Joel watched Kennedy's shoulders ease. "You went to your mommy?"

"I did," he said with confidence. "Sometimes you just need your mommy. Besides, she's quite the Kennedy advocate. She likes you a lot."

Kennedy eased against him, and he put his arm around her shoulders. "I like your mother too. She's genuine, and sweet. She loves her family too. I don't think she was selling me on you, but I think her admiration of her husband and children just comes across well by the way she speaks of you."

He thought about how his mother talked about his father and his new mower.

Joel pressed a kiss to the side of Kennedy's head. "She's happy that I've fallen in love with you."

The words were out, and he wondered what kind of response he was going to get as Kennedy eased away from him and let his arm fall from her shoulders.

"She's happy you've fallen in love with me? What the hell does that mean?"

"It means I need to choose my words more carefully. I didn't mean to freak you out."

"Freak me out? This whole day is freaking me out."

"Then let's just go back to the part where I'm here to comfort and support you, and forget about what my mother said."

"If your mother said that, then she has reason to have said it," Kennedy argued.

"Well of course she has reason to have said it. She's a really smart woman."

He watched as Kennedy bit down on her quivering lip. "You love me?"

"I think I do."

"That's a lot to take in."

"I know it is. So let's just leave it on the table. Let's go back inside, and we can pick this conversation back up some other time."

Joel stood and started for the doors. What had he gotten himself into?

He heard Kennedy's phone chime, and he turned to watch her read the text that had just come in.

"He's out of surgery. Paige said they're taking him to recovery and it'll be about an hour or so before we can see him."

"Then why don't we go to the cafeteria and take up some food. I'm sure everyone is starving."

Kennedy stood and walked toward him. "They'd all appreciate that."

Joel gave her a nod and turned back toward the door.

"Joel."

He turned when he heard her say his name. "Is your mom right? I mean, do you really feel that way?"

"I thought we were leaving this conversation for later."

She slowly walked toward him as a car pulled into the circle drive in front of the entrance. A man hurried out of the car as the doors opened again and a nurse pushed a woman out through the door in a wheelchair, a newborn infant in her arms.

The conversation had stalled as they both watched the new family settle into the car, with mom in the back seat with the newborn in its seat. The nurse waved and went back inside as the family drove away.

The whole scene squeezed at his heart and when he turned back to Kennedy, the tear she wiped away came from eyes that weren't sad.

"C'mon," he said as he took her hand, but she tugged against him until he turned back to her.

"Joel, I've never told anyone I love them. Ever. Well, aside from family. Even in the only relationship I've ever been in other than this one, I've never said it."

"And you don't have to say it now."

"I feel it though."

That lightened the ache she was creating in his chest. "Well, that's something."

"How many people have you said it to?"

Joel chuckled. "Once in sixth grade. Emily Parker was in eighth grade, and I knew that if I professed my love, she'd see me as more than her little brother's friend."

"And how did that work out?"

"She punched me."

Kennedy laughed and leaned into him. "And that was it?"

Joel bit the inside of his cheek. "There was one other. But, as I'm here having this discussion with you, you probably have concluded that that didn't work out."

Kennedy looped her arms around his neck, and he pulled her close by wrapping his arms around her waist.

"Joel, I think I feel it too. I've never felt this way about anyone, and you haven't even seen my house yet."

He wasn't sure what that was supposed to mean, but it wasn't going to change the exchange they were having. "Then let's settle on the fact that we have some seriously strong feelings, and those emotions tie us together. It's you and me. We're a unit, until the time we can say the words, or we..." He let out a breath. "Never mind. I'm not going to project something negative. I'm yours, Kennedy. I'm in it for the long haul."

This time he watched her lip quiver, and she didn't try to stop it. "I'm in too," she said. "I'm all yours, Joel."

The smile that formed on his lips came without thought. "This has been an extremely significant weekend."

"It has. You've met all of my siblings and you're about to meet my dad. Maybe you should stay at my place tonight and then you can reconsider you thoughts on the situation."

"Why would that change my mind?"

"Like I said, I'm not organized."

"All in, Kennedy."

She lifted on her toes and pressed a kiss to his lips. "All in."

CHAPTER 32

They were all huddled together in the waiting room, including Gloria, when Kennedy and Joel walked in with trays of sandwiches and chips.

"We thought everyone might be hungry," Kennedy said as Chase and Max both reached for sandwiches and Paige kept a cool eye on her.

After a moment, Paige reached for a bag of Funyuns, which Kennedy knew were her weakness in her life of proper nutrition. "Thank you," Paige bit out the words and Kennedy wondered what had gotten under her skin—besides the whole dad in surgery thing.

Conversation was minimal, and then they came with news. The surgery went well, and in heart surgery terms, it had been a standard surgery to clear a blockage. However, the entire room of people couldn't go back to see him, and they all agreed that it should be Paige, who had already started for the hallway.

Gloria fidgeted with the paper from her sandwich. "I suppose I should call around and get me a room. I have to be ready that he might not want my company after all."

Kennedy rested her hand atop of Gloria's. "He'll be happy to have you here. We can easily overwhelm, so please don't feel as if we are pushing you out."

"You've been very kind. I don't think we thought this all the way through when it happened."

"I can arrange to fly you back home—to either home," Kennedy offered.

"I think I'll stay a few days and see how things go."

Joel shifted so that he too was now in the conversation. "My brother and I own a house in the city, and we run it as an AirBnB. Currently, it is vacant. I can block it out for you."

Gloria smiled and batted tears from her eyes. "How much would that be?"

"No cost. We don't have anyone renting it right now. I'd be happy to let you stay. We don't have a reservation coming for another week."

Gloria's hand came to her lips and the tears finally fell. "Thank you. You have no idea how much I appreciate that."

Within the hour, they had all worked their way into the recovery room to see their father, and lastly Gloria had gone in. Paige had offered Chase a ride home, and Max walked out with them. Kennedy and Joel waited for Gloria so that they could take her to the rental.

"I didn't know you and your brother had an AirBnB," Kennedy said, her head rested on Joel's shoulder.

"Yeah. We actually have three. One in the city. One by the lake. One up in the mountains just off the highway for skiers."

"But currently only the one tap house?"

He snickered. "Yes. We flipped the houses and turned them into the rentals. Then we bought the other tap house and sold it within a few years. Now we have the new one."

"And you'll plan to move on and sell it?" Her words felt as heavy on her tongue as they did in her heart.

"If a buyer comes knocking. Otherwise, we run the tap house. You never think about selling your store?"

"Never," she admitted. "It's my life. Well, at least it has been."

Joel kissed the top of her head.

Kennedy went back to see her father one more time after Gloria had returned to the waiting room. He wasn't up to talking, the meds had him groggy, but the nurse thought he'd be ready to head home in a day. Kennedy knew nothing about heart surgeries. She thought a day was mighty optimistic, but that's how things were done.

Joel called his brother on the drive and told him the plans for the rental. And while he was on the phone, Jeff made it unavailable for anyone to rent. When they arrived, Joel took Gloria through the house. There was a small grocery store at the end of the block and a cozy restaurant next to that. Gloria seemed comfortable enough. Chase had agreed to pick her up the next morning and head to the hospital.

As they drove away from the rental house, Joel reached for Kennedy's hand and laced their fingers together. "This wasn't how I'd thought we'd spend our day."

She let out a ragged breath. "No, this sucked."

"I suppose you'll be heading home now?"

Kennedy turned to watch him as he drove west toward home. "I guess that's the plan. Tomorrow is Monday and I have..."

"A nail appointment first thing."

She chuckled. "I'm not much of a mystery, am I?"

"Oh, I don't know. I still have a lot to figure out. So why don't we go to my place, you get your car, and I'll meet you at your place."

Kennedy's shoulders dropped. "I'm not neat and tidy like you are."

"That was ingrained from my mother."

"Yeah, well I didn't have that. I have dishes in the sink, clothes on the floor, and expired food in my fridge. Well, not so much anymore. I did massively clean house last week."

When they had pulled to a stop light, Joel turned to her. "Do you think I'm enamored by some image of you? I get business Kennedy and casual Kennedy. I get that you're not perfect, and hell, I'm far from it. But what I don't get is that this seems to bother you a hell of a lot more than it should. Now let's consider the facts," he began as the light turned green, and he eased through the intersection. "We both work hard and sometimes work is going to get in our way. We both have families, and the dynamics are different. I've seen you naked, and yet you still worry that I'll judge you because you have clothes on the floor?"

"I can't help it. It seems to be who I am."

"Then I'll give you a thirty-minute head start," he offered as he turned down his street and pulled into his driveway. "You go home and settle the things that are making you crazy. We're only a week into this, Kennedy. Let's not throw all the kinks in at the start. We have to save something for a year from now."

That had actually made her laugh, and he knew she'd just been worked up over the day they'd had.

"I appreciate that."

"Like I said. I'm all in. I don't want to make a mess of this early on, because I think we have something good growing here."

Kennedy leaned across the cab of the truck and planted a kiss on his cheek. "I'm not even going into your house. Bring my bag with you, and a bag of your own. I'm going straight home to tidy up. I want you to walk in and assume that it's normal, even if I've told you differently."

"I can do that."

"So make it an hour," she said laughing as she opened the door. "And bring some groceries."

Joel watched as she pulled her keys from her pink purse and climbed into her car. A moment later she pulled away from his drive, and he let out a long breath. He hadn't known her but a month, but yeah, he was fully in love with her and couldn't imagine a day when she wasn't in his life.

As soon as the tap house was open, their schedules wouldn't meld anymore, then it would another obstacle for them to manage. That was okay. If what he felt was the real thing, then it would be worth the struggle.

CHAPTER 33

There was no pile on the floor of the laundry room, as Kennedy had taken care of that when she'd gone through her cleaning fit. The dishwasher was full of clean dishes and only a few dirty ones remained in the sink.

Turning on the stereo, Kennedy cranked up Van Halen, but she only cared for the Sammy Hagar era, and got to work on the slight untidiness of her house. She was fairly proud of herself, as she closed the door to her bedroom closet after having hung up the three items that had been left on the chair.

When she looked around the room, it was neat and tidy, and it hadn't been as messy as she'd had thought it was. Perhaps she was growing up, she humored. Or maybe she was happy.

The thought struck her in the chest.

She was happy.

Kennedy had never thought of herself as unhappy. She had her business. She had her friends, and she had her family. But when she thought hard about it, that was all she had. There were no dates, no trips—aside from buying trips for work—and no extra social interactions. Kennedy had become all work and no play. No wonder she put everything into her store and nothing into her outside life.

There was an emotional cloud that began to fill her head, and she recognized it. This was her pulling her emotions into a pity party, and she wasn't going to have it. The sexiest man she'd ever known—and the nicest—was thirty minutes from pulling into her driveway. He was going to sleep in her bed, and they'd get up in the morning and head off to their merry jobs.

When she thought of it that way, she had to sit on the edge of the bed.

Their jobs were very different, and though they currently ran the same hours, they wouldn't always. But if she thought too much about how things would change, Kennedy Devereaux would sabotage the new relationship she was enjoying quicker than it started.

No, she was going to give this a fair chance. After all, Joel's mother told him he was in love with her, and he hadn't denied the feelings. They were all in. They'd promised themselves that.

She heard his truck pull up to the house. Standing, she ran her hands over her clothes, and then thought she should change. No, this was all about being real.

By the time she opened the front door, Joel was walking up the front walk with two bags over his shoulders and two grocery bags, one in each arm.

Kennedy leaned against the doorjamb as casually as possible. "This is a sight I could get used to."

"Grocery delivery?"

"It's just one of the perks."

He stopped when he reached her and leaned in to kiss her gently on the lips. "You're beautiful."

"And here I was just thinking what a mess I was today."

Joel shook his head. "Quite the opposite."

Kennedy took one of the grocery bags, and her overnight bag from his shoulder and invited him into her home.

"Nice place you have here," he said as he looked around.

"Thank you." She set the grocery bag on the counter. "What did you buy?"

"Simple stuff. Spaghetti, sauce, meatballs, garlic bread, and a salad."

"I like easy."

Joel set down his bag of groceries and his overnight bag. "So, show me around."

Kennedy exchanged looks with him. "This is mostly it."

Joel raised an eyebrow then took her hand. "There's more."

With a loud sigh, Kennedy smiled. "This is the kitchen." She led him to the other room. "Living room and dining room."

"Very nice. You don't have a TV in your living room?"

"I don't watch a lot of TV. If I do, it's in my room or my jewelry room."

"Jewelry room?"

Kennedy nodded. *"Kennedy Devereaux Designs*, remember."

"Right. Show me your patio."

That was when she winced. "It's ugly."

"You worry too much."

She opened the sliding door that led to an old wooden patio that needed repair and paint.

"I don't go out here too much," she admitted. "The grass needs to be redone, as does the patio. I don't have any flowers, and only one chair."

Joel gathered her in his arms. "When I'm done building the tap house, I would love to fix up your yard. It would take a weekend at most."

"You're delusional."

"Seriously. Jeff and I could have this looking like a suburban oasis in three days max."

That was a huge offer, Kennedy thought as she leaned in closer to him. "You'd do that?"

"Of course I would." He nipped the tip of her nose with a kiss.

"Well, c'mon. I'll show you the rest."

She pointed out the small powder room just down the hall. She had to wonder what kind of magic they could do to it if they had a weekend. Maybe she'd fill her Pinterest board with ideas, just in case it ever came up in conversation.

Opening the next door down the hall, Kennedy stepped in and turned on the light.

Joel followed her in and his eyes went wide. "Wow. This is impressive."

There was a work table, with plenty of light, tools arranged by size and drawers and drawers of beads, gems, wire, clasps, and hooks.

"This is where the magic really happens."

He picked up a pair of pliers and then set them back down. "All of these pieces come together and become the jewelry in your store?"

"Yep. I get lost in here on the weekends, mostly."

Joel pulled her to him again. "I want to commission you to make something for my mother. Would you do that?"

"Of course, but I don't know her taste. I mean I know it a little, but..."

"She would love and wear anything you made for her. Seriously, she's as enamored by you as I am. And I don't care what it costs."

Ideas began to fill Kennedy's head as to what she could design. "I'll work on it."

She took his hand again and this time led him to the next room.

Joel stopped at the door as she walked in. "Very nice," he said looking into her bedroom. "This room is most like you. Feminine."

"You think so?"

"I do."

"Why are you standing way over there?" she asked, watching

him look so casual and comfortable in his own skin. She envied him that.

"Because if I walk in here I'll never want to leave. And I'm enjoying watching you in your own element."

"Dinner can wait," she offered.

Joel shook his head. "This can wait. I'm going to hold you in my arms all night long, and many nights after this. Let's go cook together. I want to pull a chair out onto your patio and have a glass of wine."

That caused her to laugh. "You certainly are an optimistic aren't you?"

"I try to be. And I'm very optimistic about us."

CHAPTER 34

*T*hey'd started something, Kennedy thought as she watched the truck of lumber back into the alley behind the tap house. She stood in the window of the break room in her store and watched Joel, his brother, and four other men unload sheets of plywood.

She didn't worry that he'd catch her now. They'd been sleeping in the same bed, between houses, for the past month. They had a routine. They had private jokes. They had each other.

"What are they bringing in now?" Hillary moved in behind Kennedy and watched. "Do you ever wonder if he's sleeping with you just so you won't be mad at the mess next door?"

Kennedy turned her head to stare at her friend. "Seriously?"

Hillary laughed. "No. He's totally taken by you, and had it been a ploy, he wouldn't have carried it this far." She poured herself a cup of coffee. "I do enjoy the breaks in here a lot more now, though. Is there anything sexier than a man in work boots?"

Kennedy hadn't given it much thought until the day she'd met Joel. But now she had to agree that it was damn sexy.

Hillary moved away from the window and picked up a muffin

from the table. "Cara is taking the baby in for her checkup, and she's going to swing by here."

"That'll be nice."

"I think she misses it, but I don't think she's coming back."

Kennedy turned to direct her attention to Hillary, leaning her hip on the counter. "I don't suppose she will. I wouldn't want her to give up being with her baby. I suppose in a month or so we should look into hiring someone new."

"I guess it wouldn't be a bad thing. Especially if you keep going with hot guy next door."

Kennedy chewed her bottom lip. "What does that have to do with what's going on in my store?"

Hillary bit into the muffin, and held up a finger to signal Kennedy to wait for the answer.

"I just mean, what you're doing now leads to things. You'll probably move in together, want to take vacations, hell, maybe you'll even get married in the next year."

"We haven't discussed that."

"I'm not saying you're discussing it. I'm saying it'll probably happen. Don't get so defensive. It's a good thing. What I'm trying to say is yes, we probably could use some help in the next few months. Kennedy Devereaux deserves to have something in her life other than this store and a list of worries about her family. Speaking of your family. How's your dad?"

The change in subject had Kennedy scrambling for words. "He's fine. That woman, Gloria, has been staying with him the past month. But she's headed back to Minnesota for a few months and then back to Miami for the winter."

Hillary nodded as she took another bite of the muffin in her hand. "Well, that'll be one less thing for you to fret over." She took one more big bite and finished the muffin. Turning, she threw the paper away in the trash and carried her coffee to the other room.

Kennedy stood in the kitchen and worried over her coffee. In a matter of moments Hillary's comments had taken her mood from joyous to pitiful.

Was he really sleeping with her to keep her happy?

Was she looking for marriage?

Did she fret over her family that much?

When Gloria left, would Kennedy be in charge of making sure Dad was taken care of?

She turned back toward the window and watched as another truck pulled up, and they began to unload buckets of paint and boxes of tile.

The tap house would be done by the end of August, just like they'd planned. And then what? If Hillary was right, and Joel was just keeping her as a happy neighbor, would it all be over?

Kennedy sipped her now bitter coffee and then dumped it in the sink. No, she refused to believe that it was all a ploy. If it was, they wouldn't be sharing a bed every night. Their relationship would have stayed in a place of friendly dating. This was more—so much more.

Joel walked out to the truck and looked up at the window. He smiled up at her, and she felt the warmth of it fill her. Hillary had just stirred her up. That was all.

IF THEY KEPT the pace they were keeping, they'd have the tap room ready by the end of August and a grand opening party by Labor Day. Joel's sister-in-law lived for planning big parties. It would be extraordinary.

The thought that he'd have Kennedy on his arm the entire night only made it that much more exciting. Sure, he'd be working too, but she'd be there.

"Hey, jackass, would you hand me that nail gun?" his brother's voice shook him from his thoughts. He handed him the tool. "Thank you. What the hell is in your head this morning?"

"Just thinking about our progress and the party your wife is planning."

"Well, if we don't get this done, there won't be a party, so keep your head in the game."

Joel sat back on his heels as his brother tacked in the base board they were working on. "What do you think of Kennedy. I mean, be honest."

His brother shot him an unamused glare before finishing the nailing, then turned to him, sitting back on his heels just as Joel was.

"Seriously? You want a heart-to-heart when we already know we'll be here until midnight?"

"You're right. Never mind," Joel agreed and pulled the next board over.

"Shit." Jeff stood and walked to the cooler for two bottles of water and returned with them. He pushed a bucket over next to Joel, handed him one of the bottles of water, and sat down on the inverted bucked. "You're in love with her and now you're getting all mushy."

Joel laughed as he twisted the top off of his bottle. "I can't help it."

"She's good people, as mom would say. And mom absolutely loves her. She's a good judge of people."

"She loved Audrey too."

"Because Audrey is good people too, you just didn't work out."

"Sure didn't." Joel took a long drink. "What if Kennedy is just as strong headed."

Jeff laughed as he wiped his mouth with the back of his hand. "Kennedy is more strong headed, she's just planted here. You can't go comparing your one failed relationship with the one you're working on. You'll never get anywhere. Sure, when I first met Kennedy I thought she'd be a snob. I was wrong. Very wrong."

"I am in love with her."

"Not news."

"I want to marry her."

Jeff nodded. "I figured this was where that was going. You're worried about how she'll feel about it?"

Joel shrugged. "Can't help but be worried. It's only been a few months."

"Yeah, but you're not some spring chicken. You're getting old, bud." They both laughed and finished off their bottles of water. "Besides, when you know, you know. I proposed to Dina after we'd known each other four months."

"You were together for three years before you got married."

Jeff stood from the bucket and tossed his bottle into the trash. "I proposed, she said yes, and we even talked about eloping. We changed our minds on that. I planned a big proposal in front of everyone a year and a half into our relationship and it satisfied everyone—including Dina. She'd always wanted engagement photos. I gave her a different ring, so the pictures are genuine," he said smiling.

Joel twisted the cap onto his bottle and off again. "I was thinking of proposing to her on Labor Day. At the grand opening party."

"What does Mom think?"

Joel ran his tongue over his teeth. "She's the one who thinks I should ask her."

"Like I said, she loves her."

Joel managed himself up off the ground. His knees ached from the work they'd been doing. He was glad he'd brought the subject up, even if his brother hadn't wanted to talk about it. But now he was sure about what he wanted to do.

CHAPTER 35

*K*ennedy noticed Joel's truck was gone when she'd left work. As they were getting further along with the remodel, his hours had gotten later.

They'd made a schedule, because they both found that they enjoyed making schedules, to stay at one another's houses. Keys, garage door codes, and alarm passwords had been exchanged.

Tonight they were staying at Joel's, so Kennedy would head over after begrudgingly attending one of her sister's yoga classes. She owed it to Paige to show up regularly every week. After all, Paige was Kennedy's first employee and the job hadn't paid well.

Joel had ordered groceries, and wouldn't be home until late, so Kennedy had planned on a night in his jetted tub, a glass of wine, and just a small salad for dinner. There was a Hallmark movie on that she wanted to watch, and his bed had big fluffy pillows.

She laughed as she drove toward his house. His house was like a retreat. Maybe if things went well between them, and it became forever, they could live at his house. It was much nicer.

When she turned the corner she noticed his truck in the

driveway. Had she misunderstood that he was going to be working late? Maybe something had happened.

Kennedy pulled into the driveway, next to his truck, and hurried into the house. No, there couldn't be anything wrong. Music played and the scents coming from the kitchen made her mouth water.

She dropped the keys in the bowl by the door and walked in.

"I thought you were working late," she said, and he turned.

Her heartbeat quickened looking at him with his scruffy beard, no shirt, and a kitchen towel draped over his shoulder.

"I was going to, but there were more important things to tend to."

Kennedy moved toward the island and pulled out one of the bar stools and took a seat. "More important than getting your business open?"

Joel nodded as he reached for a wine glass and filled it with the bottle he had next to the stove. "I wanted to spend my night with you. Thankfully I have a brother who loves his wife enough to understand what I needed to do."

Kennedy kept a narrow gaze on him as she took the glass he offered, then watched as he walked around the island and stood in front of her.

Joel lifted his hands to her face. "God, you're beautiful."

"What's going on?" She hoped her voice carried a little humor, but she wasn't sure she felt it.

"I just couldn't wait to have you in my arms." He pressed a kiss to her lips and eased back.

"Everything's okay?"

"Everything's perfect," he agreed as he took the glass of wine and set it on the counter. Taking her hands he pulled her to her feet. "That has to simmer."

She admired his half-dressed body, clad in only jeans. His feet were bare which made him even more casual. She noticed his hair was getting a little long, and she figured this was what he'd look like when he was fully engaged in a project, like the tap room.

He led her to the sofa and eased her down under him, his mouth working against hers, driving up her temperature. When his lips moved to her throat, she tangled her fingers in his hair and found she enjoyed the extra length. It was sexy.

"This isn't how I thought I'd be spending my evening," she said breathlessly.

"This is better?"

"So much better."

"Good." His mouth was on hers again, and then he eased back. "Because there's something I want to tell you."

"And this is how you wanted to tell me? A text wouldn't work?"

He chuckled. "It's something I wanted to revisit from a month or so ago."

"And what's that?"

Joel hovered over her. His dark eyes fixed on hers. "We started this conversation once, a month ago, and I just wanted to have it again."

Now she laughed. "Are you talking in code?"

A smile settled on his lips. "I love you, Kennedy Devereaux. I love you."

She sucked in a breath and replayed the words in her head. Yes, they most certainly had this conversation before, but now things were different. There was more at stake now.

They weren't just fooling around, and well, she knew that. But what about what Hillary had said? Was there any merit to that?

Joel eased back more. "Do you have anything you want to say?"

Kennedy opened her mouth and then closed it again. This was it. This was the moment she decided if she was going to use the words. She hadn't when he'd first brought it up, but now it was all different.

"I...I..." Her mouth had gone dry and Joel eased back even further.

"You're not ready to go there yet."

The look of disappointment on his face twisted in her gut.

"I wasn't expecting that," she admitted.

He nodded as he sat up and moved off of her to sit on the sofa. "The element of surprise isn't good for you. I get that."

"You're right. I don't do well with surprise."

"So I should have written this all out and scheduled it on your planner? Should I highlight that in yellow or pink?"

She was wise enough to know she'd hurt his feelings, but now he was taking digs at her. They were treading on unfamiliar ground here too. Did she tell him she loved him or did she walk out? She'd never done either, and she didn't know what this called for.

Joel pushed himself to his feet and went back to the kitchen. He continued working at the stove and Kennedy watched.

Why was this so hard? Just because she'd never used the words before didn't mean she didn't feel them. Just because her father didn't understand commitment didn't mean she wouldn't. She had no doubt in her mind that Joel understood commitment. His parents were the poster children for marriage.

Marriage, that wasn't what he'd said.

He'd said he loved her, and she froze up and didn't even dig deep enough to wrap her head around what she felt.

"Joel," she said as she stood, but he didn't turn. Walking to the kitchen, she moved in behind him, wrapping her arms around his waist and pressing her cheek to his back. "Don't give up on me. I'm figuring this out."

"Yeah, so am I."

"I'm not easy to get along with."

"Now I figured that out the moment I met you standing outside your store. I'm still here, sweetheart."

That seemed to sting a little, his use of sweetheart with a bite in it.

"Are you sleeping with me so that I won't be a pain in your ass over all the construction noise?"

That had him setting down the spoon and turning to look at her. "Excuse me?"

No, Hillary was wrong. Kennedy could see it in his eyes. She'd crossed the line and now she wondered how she could cross back.

Kennedy shook her head and pressed her fingers to her temples. "I'm sorry. I shouldn't have said that."

"Saying it is one thing. Did you mean it? Do you think that's what we're doing? Do you think I would tell you that if all I wanted was to keep you from complaining?"

"No. No. It's just something that was said to me, and it stuck in my head."

"Who said it? I'd like to have a word with them."

For some reason that calmed her. No, she wouldn't tell him who said it, because she didn't think Hillary meant it either.

"I'm sorry. I'm so sorry."

Joel moved to her and placed his hands on her face. "Don't be sorry, about any of this. You're not ready to tell me you love me. I get it. I'm ready to tell you. The feeling was so overwhelming that I ditched my team to be here to tell you." He eased back so he could look at her. "I don't need the words, Kennedy. I have you right here and I know you feel it, even if you can't call it out."

Joel turned and picked up the spoon again and Kennedy walked to where he'd set her wine. She took a sip, and then another.

"I do love you," she said, and he turned his head slightly to acknowledge her. "God," she sighed as she took another sip of her wine. "I have never, ever said that before."

"How does it feel?"

"Scares me to death," she laughed. "But I mean it. I know that I love you. I know that the reason you're sleeping with me, and we're pretty much living together is because you love me too. I love everything about you." The words were coming easier now. "I love you, Joel Kingsley."

Now he laughed as he set the spoon down and turned the heat down on the stove. He moved to her swiftly taking her mouth with his. His hand cupped the back of her neck and her heart began to race again.

A moment later he hitched her up to his waist, and she wrapped her legs around him as he carried her down the hall to his bedroom. She never did find out what had smelled so good in the kitchen.

CHAPTER 36

For the first time since she'd opened her store, Kennedy Devereaux walked in after it had been opened.

When she pushed open the back door she was met with three sets of angry eyes. Hillary's, Paige's, and Chase's.

"Good morning, crew. What's going on?" she asked as she set her bag on a chair.

Chase folded his arms over his chest. "Something wrong with your car?"

"No. Why?"

"You drove in with Joel."

"I did. I'm fairly sure you all know I'm seeing him, and we're staying with each other. So we thought it would be nice to drive in together."

Paige took a step forward. "Something wrong with your phone?"

Kennedy pulled it from her purse and looked down at it. "Yep, I didn't charge it. It appears to be dead."

Now it was Hillary's turn. "Perhaps those would be good details to keep track of considering you've never, ever been late."

"I'm here before my first client."

"You've never, ever been late," Hillary reminded her.

"So you're all standing here because you're worried about me? That's very sweet."

Paige shook her head. "It's irritating actually. We depend on you to be a certain way, and we don't know what to think when you're not."

Kennedy couldn't help but laugh at how silly that sounded. "You're all mad because I wasn't where I was supposed to be when you expected me to be there? Should I remind you all that you've all done this to me for years? How about that time, Paige, when you ran away from home for a week and went on vacation with friends when you were seventeen? And Chase and Hillary, do I need to remind you about…"

She didn't get the words out before Hillary held up a finger. "Don't even go there."

Chase exchanged looks with both of them. "Yeah, don't even go there."

The back door opened and Joel stepped through, but stopped abruptly when he saw the faces on the people scolding Kennedy.

"Did I interrupt something?" He stepped fully inside.

"I'm just in trouble for not charging my phone or being the first one here," Kennedy explained and exchanged looks with the rest of them. "Would you like to tell them that I'm not in any danger and that you love me and wouldn't hurt me?"

Joel cleared his throat and Chase shook his head. "Get used to this," Chase warned. "She'll call you out on your shit."

Joel nodded as he stood next to Kennedy. "I'm well aware. Anyway, my sister-in-law just dropped off the invitations for the grand opening. We should be open the last week of August, but the grand opening is Labor Day." He handed them each an invitation and gave one to Kennedy as well. "We'd love to have you all there."

Chase studied the invitation. "I'll make sure to have drivers on call that night. I'll be there. Can I bring a date?"

"Of course."

Hillary fanned herself with the invitation and gave Chase a glance. "I'll bring a date too. I'll know the name of my date, but that's not a prerequisite, right?"

Kennedy watched as Joel's mouth opened and closed.

Like a mother herding small children out of the kitchen, she shooed them to the other room and then wrapped her arms around Joel's neck.

"I'm sorry about them. They're a little unpredictable."

He pulled her in closely. "They love you and watch out for you. And what's with Hillary and Chase?"

"One night stand gone wrong."

"Really? Hillary and Chase?"

"You saw me pull him out of his house with a woman in his bed. Why does this surprise you?"

"The Hillary part surprises me."

Kennedy rested her head on his shoulder. "Yeah, it surprised me too when I found them." She wanted to change the subject. "So this is going to be a big deal party?"

"Dina only does big deal parties. I have more invitations. Invite your mom and her husband, as well as Max."

"I will."

"What else were they giving you a hard time over?"

Kennedy drew in a deep breath. "I drove in with you and I didn't charge my phone."

"Problematic."

"Seems to have been."

Joel rested his hands on her hips and eased her back to look at her. "Well, here's something else to contemplate today. One, my mother has an appointment with you at two o'clock. She's texted me three times to tell me she'd be next door."

"She must have scheduled with Hillary."

"She's excited. But that's not the part I want you to contemplate. Don't say anything now. But what do you think about us moving in together?"

Kennedy took a breath and Joel pressed his fingertips to her lips.

"Don't answer me now. Just think it over. Either house, or one we choose. But I think I'd like to take that next step." Kennedy nodded her head, fully aware that her mouth was wide open. Joel kissed her cheek. "I love you. I'll see you later."

He turned and walked back out of the door as Kennedy watched him walk away from the window.

"Wow," Hillary's voice came from the doorway. "That's big."

"You heard all of that?"

"I heard the I love you."

Kennedy felt the heat rise in her cheeks. "He wants me to think about moving in together."

"He's serious about you. Love and the move in? That's big, Ken. Big."

"His mother is coming in today."

"That's what I just came to tell you. She wants to look at that red jacket and that blue suit. She said to pick her out three or four more outfits to look at. She also wants something nice for the grand opening party."

Kennedy pressed her hand to her chest. "This is it, isn't it? This is real? Like the real thing?"

Hillary moved to her and wrapped her arms around her. "This is it, my friend. True love has finally found you. Hold on tight and don't let it go."

CHAPTER 37

$\mathcal{B}$y the time that June Kingsley strolled through the front door of her store, Kennedy was prepared.

"Mrs. Kingsley, it's so very nice to see you," Kennedy met her at the front. "I was thrilled to see you on my books today."

"I couldn't wait to get back in here, and please call me June."

Her eyes sparkled like Joel's, Kennedy thought, and she wondered if his children's eyes would sparkle like that too. The very thought made her dizzy, and she had to push the image of children from her mind.

"Hillary gave me the rundown on the items you wanted to see. I've pulled out some pieces for you in the back. Would you like a glass of wine?"

"That would be wonderful."

Kennedy exchanged glances with Hillary, who nodded.

Kennedy escorted June to the back room where she'd prepared the area with items she knew she would love. That was part of the service. She was examining a blouse when Hillary brought them each a glass of wine and winked at Kennedy before pulling the curtain closed.

"I never like to drink alone," June said as she sipped her wine. "Everything here is so beautiful."

Kennedy noticed the bracelet on her wrist. "I see Joel gave you the bracelet."

June turned, again her eyes sparkling. "He did. He said he'd asked you to make it just for me. I don't own anything quite as beautiful. And I mean that. My husband was never into buying me jewelry, and my mother didn't have many pieces. Knowing that my son asked for you to make this and you coordinated it with me in mind, that's a precious gift."

"I don't think I've ever had anyone appreciate something in quite that way."

"It's true. Now, let's find me something casual and stunning for their grand opening. Dina's parents are going to take the kids for the night, so I'll be able to join the evening. Last time they opened a tap house, I watched the grandkids and Dina's parents went to the party."

"So it's a big deal, huh?"

"It's always a big deal when your children do something amazing. I know it's just another night at work for them, but it's a night to celebrate. Considering those two could argue when they were little, it's fun to see them work together and build things that they love. The tap houses and the rental houses they flip. Who knew they'd grow up to be so good with their hands."

"Did they build things when they were little?"

June held up another blouse and examined it in the mirror. "There is a tree house in the back yard that they built with their father. It still stands and the grandkids play in it. Jeff was always tearing apart electronics and Joel would build boxes," she humored. "I have a lot of special boxes."

June decided on a few pieces to try on, and Kennedy waited for her to emerge from the fitting room. The image of Joel presenting his mother with a handmade box filled her heart. She didn't have anything like that with her siblings. Yes, she and Max grew up in the same house, but they weren't alike at all. She was creative and he was too analytical. Chase did his own thing and Paige was much younger than they were. Wouldn't it have been nice to have had a partner, like Joel did?

When his mother walked out of the dressing room, Kennedy's eyes welled with tears.

June hurried to her. "Oh, sweetheart. Is everything okay?"

Kennedy brushed away the tears and laughed. "Is it silly that I'm overwhelmingly jealous of what your boys had. And when you talk about them," she pressed her hands to her chest. "I can't think of another woman I've ever seen or talked to that admires her family the way you do."

June took Kennedy's hands in her own. "My mother raised six of us, alone. My father died when my youngest sister was born. I never wanted for anything—but normality. When I met Tim I knew he could give that to me. My mother did everything she could, and I had an amazing childhood, but under the circumstances she was a little bitter toward us. My boys are my everything, and their father, he's included in that. It's something wonderful to have someone love you."

And Kennedy knew what that was like. She had that now, and yet she second guessed everything about it.

June turned to examine herself in the mirror. "Joel says he asked you to move in with him."

"He told you that?"

"There isn't much he doesn't tell me. Nothing personal, mind you." June brushed her hands down the front of the blouse. "I can guarantee you that wherever you call home, Joel will make it nice, and no doubt you'll make it beautiful."

"You don't think it's a bad idea? Or rushed?"

"When you know, you know. Right?" She turned in the mirror again. "I want this one, and do you have it in blue also?"

KENNEDY STOOD at the back door of the tap house and looked inside. She'd done her best to stay out of the way when it came to Joel's progress. What she hadn't realized was just how much they'd gotten done.

The floors were done and the walls she hadn't helped him paint were now painted. Paint cans were stacked in the corner for the up and coming finish to the room.

The bar was in place, and they'd made the right choice to keep the mail boxes. Kennedy thought they added a nice touch.

"We don't open for a few more weeks," she heard Joel's voice from across the room.

"That's a shame," she said sauntering to the center of the room. "I could use a drink."

Joel reached for her hand and began to sway to the music playing behind the bar on an old speaker. "Did you have a nice day at work, dear?"

"I did. I had the nicest client. She talks about her children and her husband all the time. She loves them dearly."

Joel spun her in a circle. "They must be some dynamite people."

"I admire your mother."

"And she admires you."

"I'll move in with you," Kennedy blurted out the words and Joel stopped their impromptu dance.

"You will?"

Kennedy nodded. "When you know, you know. Right?"

"You did talk to my mother." He pressed a kiss to her lips. "I'll make you very happy. I promise."

"Don't promise. Promises are easily broken. Let's just take this one step at a time and work on it."

"I think we should celebrate," he began to sway with her in his arms again.

"How?"

Joel stopped again. "I have some ideas, but let's go get Mexican food again, like we did on our first date."

"That wasn't a date."

"It counts. Let's go have dinner and then go home. I want to make arrangements to move."

"We didn't decide where yet."

"It doesn't matter. We'll live in one house and rent out the other."

Kennedy hadn't thought of that, but of course Joel would. "I like your house better than mine," she admitted.

"What's mine is yours."

"We can make arrangements after Labor Day. Once the doors to this place are open."

Joel pulled her close and pressed his lips to hers. "I don't want to wait. Bring a box over every night, and it'll be as if you're already there."

And as he swayed with her in his arms some more, Kennedy knew this was that forever she'd been avoiding. Hillary was right. This was it, and she was going to hold on tight.

CHAPTER 38

*H*illary had agreed to stay later on Saturday nights to help clean the store so that Kennedy could focus all of her efforts on packing on Sundays.

She'd taken all the broken down boxes they'd accumulated over the past two weeks, as well as whatever Joel had saved up. The plan was to pack a few boxes after work and take what she could carry in her car over to Joel's.

They were getting down to the wire at the tap house and his hours grew later and later. There had been quite a few nights where she stayed in her own home packing more boxes because she knew she'd be alone if she went to his house.

It threw a little kink in their plan to be together more, but she understood the deadlines of business and what it took to get the door open. Soon enough he'd be with her all the time.

Kennedy sat on the floor of her bedroom sorting out her clothes. She realized that one of the things that had changed was the time she spent in her closet, now that she'd rather spend her time with Joel. There had been a time that hours would be spent planning and accessorizing outfits, after all, it was part of her job. But it was more than that. She loved looking pretty and distinguished. Just the day before, she and Hillary had finalized her travel itinerary for fashion week in September. She'd attend in New York this year, and fly to Paris for February's shows.

That wasn't something she and Joel had had much discussion about. New York's shows were too close to his opening for him to go with her, but maybe in February they could make a vacation out of it.

When her phone buzzed in her pocket, she pulled it out.

It was a text from her father. Are you home? I'm on your front porch.

Kennedy laughed as she pushed herself to her feet and limped to the front door, her numb legs threatening to give out beneath her.

Her father stood on the front porch, a bag of Chinese food in his hands. "Do you have time for me and some dinner?"

"Of course. Don't you think that your eating that is why you had a heart attack?"

He winked and walked past her to the kitchen. "Gloria had me on a low carb healthy diet. She left explicit instructions. I needed something else."

Her father set the food on the table and pulled out two sets of chopsticks. He handed her a set and pulled the paper off of the other. Opening the boxes he set them out so they could take a little out of each and Kennedy gathered paper plates to eat from, as she'd already packed up her dishes.

"She stayed longer than I thought she would," Kennedy admitted.

"I asked her to. I mean it. It was nice to have her around."

As her father took the first bite of his food she watched his eyes. They were sad, and she wondered when they'd become that way. Was it possible he was lonely without Gloria there? Had he been that way before too? Had she just been as lonely and not noticed it?

With his mouth full of noodles, her father looked around. "Are you packing?"

Kennedy laughed as she poured out a few pieces of orange chicken and set a dumpling on her plate.

"Yes. I'm moving in with Joel."

Her father's eyes shifted up as if he were trying to remember. "He was at the hospital."

"Yes."

"He's the one that let Gloria stay in his rental house?"

"Yes."

"Must be a very patient guy."

That jab was a little too sharp. "Why do you say that?"

"To move in with you. You like things a certain way. You like to be in control. I'm just saying, that takes a special person. A patient person. You're a lot like your mother."

Kennedy bit down on a piece of chicken so hard she thought she might have cracked her tooth. "Did you come here to start a fight? I'm not interested in that. You might have had troubles living with mom—obviously—but that doesn't translate to my relationship."

Her father set his chopsticks across the plate and clasped his hands under his chin. "You know what, that was rude of me. No, I didn't come here to pick a fight."

"Why did you come here?" she asked and then wish she hadn't. After the whole heart attack episode, she didn't need to question him coming around. She needed to appreciate every moment she had with him.

"I came because you're smart."

"I'm smart? What does that have to do with anything?"

He chuckled and picked back up his chopsticks. "It's just that you think things through. I want to keep seeing Gloria."

"Then by all means you should do that. This is the age of internet dating."

"I know, and I'm learning. Online sex is something, huh?"

Kennedy stopped chewing mid bite when she felt the bile rise in her throat. "Seriously, let's not even go there."

"Right. I'm thinking of going to Miami to see her. I mean we already have plans for that."

"I knew that."

"I've just been thinking, the cruise was a big step for me. You know, getting out and meeting people. Maybe it's time for me to think about the next part of my life. Do I want to stay here, or should I go see the world? Should I spend some time in Miami? There's nothing really for me here."

Again, his words pierced her. "Me. Chase. Max. Paige," her voice had risen.

"And all you do is take care of me. Paige is all grown up, she doesn't need me like she did. Chase and Max, they never did need me looking over their shoulders. And you, well, you have someone now. Explore that."

"It doesn't mean I want you to go."

Her father reached his hand across the table and placed it on hers. "When I have grandkids I'll make sure I'm here. I think it's time for me to see what's out there."

When her father left, Kennedy crawled into bed and contemplated the conversation they'd had. Kennedy held what her father did to her mother too close to her heart. That was thirty-six years ago. They'd both grown since then, and other than having a child with his mistress, she groaned, he'd stepped up and had been an exceptional father. He was right. All of his kids were grown and doing their thing. Paige was on her own, and she too was doing what she wanted to do. Maybe it was time for him to try something new, just like she was.

Kennedy closed her eyes and blocked out the mess that surrounded her. In a few weeks, she'd wake up with Joel in their shared bed every day... for the rest of her life.

CHAPTER 39

They were one week from opening and inspections were taking too long. Joel sorted through invoices that had just come in while Oliver and Craig fixed the taps behind the bar.

Jeff was out back with another inspector and Dina had the kids sitting at one of the tables coloring while she tapped out party plans on her laptop.

"That's one more off the list," Jeff announced as he waved the signed inspection sheet in the air.

"It would be nice if they all kept their appointments and showed up when they said they were going to," Joel bit out. "Where's our occupancy approval?"

"Tomorrow at eight o'clock."

This was how it had worked the last time too, but for some reason, the process was wearing on Joel's nerves a little more.

Jeff sat down at the chair next to him and held out his hands for his daughter to run toward him with the picture she'd drawn for him.

"Daddy, this is you and Uncle Joel. You're making beer," she said as she showed him the picture.

"Is this Uncle Joel with no hair?" he teased by kicking Joel under the table.

"He has on a hat," she corrected him.

"Oh. I like it. Is it done? Can I hang it up?"

"I'll add more to it," she said as she jumped down and ran back to the other table.

Jeff leaned back in his chair. "You gotta get you some of those." He nodded toward his family and Joel pulled his attention from the invoices to watch.

"Someday."

"Are you still going to ask her to marry you?"

"Why wouldn't I? I have her living in my house. I love her. Things are just moving along."

"I heard you already have someone interested in leasing her house."

Joel nodded. "We'll get her moved in fully after Labor Day. Then first of October, we'll have it leased out."

"I can't believe you're getting married."

"She didn't say yes yet."

"I won't start a pool on how long this one will last," Jeff teased and it was Joel's turn to kick him under the table.

The front door of Kennedy's store opened as she and Hillary stood behind the counter creating price tags for the new bags that had just arrived. Joel, Jeff, Oliver, and Craig all walked in and stood in front of them with enormous grins.

"Gentlemen, how can I help you? I don't think I have your sizes, but…"

Craig was the first to laugh.

Joel reached his hand across the counter for her to take it. When she did, he guided her around the counter to stand with him.

"We would like to invite you to be our first guests at the Kingsley Tap House."

"You got all of your inspections and licenses and whatever!"

"We did," he said as he pulled her in close. "We have beer in our taps and food trucks scheduled to begin serving Thursday. We'll call that our soft opening. Next weekend we'll have our party. And then, we're a staple of Olde Town, ready to bring business to the square. But the first drink is on us. Can you ladies take a break?"

Kennedy looked around the store. Mondays were for stocking, and they had their share of it to do. But much like being late to work, she'd never closed up to take a break in the middle of the day either. This was cause to do just that.

"I think we could hang a sign on the door and come to have a celebration drink."

Hillary pulled a piece of blank paper from the printer and quickly made a sign. A few minutes later, they had locked up, and walked next door to celebrate the achievement of the Kingsley brothers and their partners.

It was the first time Kennedy had walked through the front door of the tap house, and the aesthetics were different, as they were meant to be. The tables were spaced out and had chairs around them. There were a few benches that lined the walls and a digital jukebox in the corner. Glasses were lined up on the wall each of them with the Kingsley Tap House logo etched into them.

Jeff had moved around the bar and had two glasses poised and ready to fill.

"What'll it be?" He pointed to the chalkboard that had been beautifully decorated.

Hillary made noises as she decided. "I want that citrus one."

"Coming up," Jeff said as he pulled it from the tap. He slid the beer to Hillary and then shifted his attention to Kennedy. "I've been told you liked the coffee and chocolate beer."

"I did."

"I have it on tap."

"Then I'll take it," she said as she watched her brothers walk through the door. "What are you two doing here?"

Chase grinned. "We were told free beer. Why wouldn't we be here?"

She kissed each of them as they stood next to the bar looking up at the menu.

A moment later her father and sister walked in. She couldn't believe Joel had called her entire family to have a beer.

She sat down with Oliver and Craig. Then they pulled more tables together as Jeff greeted his parents at the door and kissed them both. They were followed by Dina and the kids.

Kennedy's heart swelled at the sight of Jeff with a kid in each arm. They, too, made their way to the bar and Jeff opened them each a bottle of soda.

When the tables had all been moved and more chairs added, Kennedy realized that Joel wasn't around, and as she moved off of her stool she saw her mother and step-father walk in as well.

She walked toward them. "What are you doing here?" She kissed each of them, and was pleased when her father stood to shake her step-father's hand and kiss her mother on the cheek as well.

"Joel called and said they'd gotten permission to open and that we should drop by. So here we are."

And that was when she saw him come through the front door, just as the others had, though she'd never seen him leave. He carried a box in his hands, one that looked as if it had been hand-made from scraps of wood. Perhaps one of the boxes his mother had talked about.

"Come here," he said with a nod of his head, and she followed him back to the table where she'd been sitting.

Jeff poured her mother and step-father each a glass, and they sat down with what she realized was mostly her family.

Joel set the box on the table and waited for her to take her seat before he took his.

"I made this box for my mother thirty years ago," he said, and she thought it resembled something a seven-year-old would have put together. "She's kept it all these years."

"Because she loves you," Kennedy said, and she heard June sigh from across the table.

"She does. She loves you too," he continued and when Kennedy looked toward her, June nodded. "But on this momentous occasion, she told me I could give it to you. It was the start of my career of building things, and it seemed like the right thing to give you for new beginnings too."

It was then Kennedy realized that everyone had gone quiet.

"Thank you," she said, not sure why he'd want her to have the old box.

"When I gave my mom the box, I'd put dandelions in it." Everyone had a small laugh. "But I put something in there for you."

Kennedy's mouth went dry and her hands began to shake.

Joel draped an arm over her shoulders. "Open it."

Unsure of what he was doing, she carefully lifted the lid and the tears began to stream down her cheeks without warning when she saw the ring centered in the box. A pink stone encircled with diamonds.

Lifting her hand to her trembling lips, Kennedy batted the tears from her eyes.

"Joel, it's beautiful."

"*Kennedy Pink*. Anything else just wouldn't be right." He lifted it from the box. "But it comes with more. The new beginning I was talking about is more than this place or you moving in. Kennedy, will you marry me?"

Her throat closed, and she couldn't even make a sound let alone let words flow.

He'd made sure everyone that was important to her was in that room at that moment. He'd had a ring designed just for her. He'd asked her to marry him.

"What do you think? You and me forever?" he asked, and then held the ring at the tip of her finger waiting for an answer.

She still couldn't make the words come out, so she nodded.

That was when she saw the tears roll from his eyes.

"That's a yes, right?"

Kennedy managed to squeak out a yes, but she wasn't sure anyone but Joel heard it. He slid the beautiful ring on her finger and pulled to him and kissed her.

CHAPTER 40

*I*n the moonlight that cascaded through the window, Kennedy held her hand up to admire the ring on her finger. She'd never seen anything so beautiful, and she was a designer of beautiful things.

"I've never seen a ring that complemented a finger more than that one," Joel said as he reached for her hand and pressed a kiss to it.

Kennedy rolled against him, her naked skin touching his. Their bodies contoured to one another as if they'd been created that way. "Never in my entire life did I think that someone would ask me to marry them."

"I'm just lucky no one got to you before I did. And I know you don't like surprises, but…"

Pressing a kiss to his chest, Kennedy lifted her hand to admire the ring again. "I'll let this one slide," she humored.

"I guess now we need to set a date."

"I had been thinking that when I go to Paris in February, you could go with me. We could make it a honeymoon now."

Joel's fingers softly caressed her shoulder. "I've never been to Paris."

"It's beautiful. You'll appreciate the architecture."

"So a late January, early February wedding?"

Kennedy closed her eyes. "February sounds romantic, doesn't it?"

"I suppose it does."

"When I get back from New York, then we'll settle on a date. A solid date."

Joel pulled his arm out from under Kennedy, and rolled so that he hovered above her. "I don't know about you going to New York. How am I supposed to survive one day without you here?"

"I'll FaceTime you all the time. Besides, you'll be busy working that new business of yours."

"That's right. It'll be time for me to work behind the bar. I suppose I'll remember how I did that before." he kissed her neck and Kennedy closed her eyes. "So many things to think about, but there is only one thing on my mind. So for now, everything else can wait. Kissing every inch of your body is all I have planned for the rest of the night."

THERE WAS a feeling that surged through Kennedy every time she looked down at her hand. The emails on her computer sat there because she couldn't be bothered with them. Her coffee had gone cold, because she was staring at the ring on her finger.

"That's some fancy news I heard," Cara's voice took Kennedy from her thoughts.

Cara held her sleeping daughter to her chest as she sat in the chair next to Kennedy's desk.

Kennedy held out her hand to show off the beautiful ring. "Have you ever seen anything so beautiful?"

"Well…" Cara nodded toward her daughter. "Kennedy, it's beautiful. I'm so happy for you. When I left, I had no idea your entire life was about to change."

"Neither did I. Seriously, when I met him I wasn't even being nice."

"Things have a way of changing. That's why I'm here." Cara rubbed her hand down her daughter's back. "I can't come back. I thought I could, but…"

"Say no more. You wanted that baby so much, and you went through so much to have her. You should always think of her first. Someday she'll go to school, and you'll need a distraction. Then we can talk."

Cara laughed. "I'll be sending mine off to school and you'll be having some."

"Well, I don't know about that. It took me this long to find a man. I'm running out of time for the other part."

"I don't think so. You're not as old as you think you are." Her daughter stirred in her arms and she shifted her. "Would you like to hold her?"

There was a stirring inside of Kennedy when Cara handed her daughter to her. The softness. The smell. The sensation.

Children had never been on Kennedy's radar—ever. But at that moment, knowing she had the right man, she couldn't imagine not having them.

"That looks good on you," Joel said as he stood in the doorway. "Hey, Cara. You look good, too."

"Thanks," she accepted the compliment. "And congratulations. You got a ring on that finger."

"I did," he beamed as he said it. "Can I hold her? I promise that I'm clean."

Cara nodded and Kennedy handed him the baby.

He didn't seem near as awkward holding her. There was a naturalness to him, but then again he'd been around kids. He had a niece and a nephew. But when he smiled down at the sweet face looking up at him, her heart melted. She would certainly give this man a baby just to see him look like that. And again, she realized his eyes sparkled, just like his mother's.

She'd been skeptical about a bar next door, but it sure had changed her world.

"I suppose we should be going. She's going to want to feed soon," Cara stood and Joel handed her the baby. "It was so good to see you both. I'm very happy for you. I can't wait to see what kind of dress you get, Kennedy. It'll be magnificent."

Cara pulled her bag over her shoulder and walked out of Kennedy's office with her baby in her arms.

"Cara came to quit," Kennedy told Joel. "She can't leave the baby. I can't blame her."

"It's a blessing when a child can have a parent at home. Even more so if it works out and both parents can be around."

"I guess our kids wouldn't have that, would they?"

He shrugged. "They could have something different. We're both in charge of our own hours. We'd just work them out so that we were with them all the time. And we'd work in our own time too. But children aren't something we've ever talked about. The subject is open for conversation?"

Kennedy sat back in her chair and crossed her legs. "Let's just say, the more I think about it, the option isn't off the table. I don't know how good of a mother I would be. But something tells me you'd be a fantastic father."

"I was lucky enough to have a good example. We'll get back to this conversation. It was nice to hold a baby again." He moved to her and pressed a kiss to the top of her head. "Speaking of kids, Joel's are sick, so I'm switching him nights. I'll be at the tap room until two o'clock."

"In the morning?"

"It's how it works."

Kennedy let out a sigh. "I guess this is the way it'll be."

"But, we have an amazing taco truck and baseball on the TVs. I would love to have a sexy blonde at the end of the bar making eyes at me while I work."

Kennedy stood, and draped her arms around his neck. "I'd better be the only sexy blonde ever catching your eye."

"Truth be told, you're the only sexy blonde that's ever caught it."

CHAPTER 41

*S*oft opening had just been a phrase, Joel thought as he worked behind the bar. They had been packed since the moment they turned on the open sign. The night he'd covered for Jeff, he'd convinced Kennedy to hang out for a few hours. What he hadn't expected to happen was her bussing tables and washing glasses, but she'd taken to the task and done it without him asking.

Every night since then, she'd just jumped in and helped. Each of the partners had decided that the night of their grand opening, they didn't want to just be working, so rather quickly, they put a makeshift staff together of friends and family. Chase had volunteered to be Joel's employee and pour for the night. Joel figured it would work to benefit Chase. Not only would he get paid and tipped, he'd meet some new women, and maybe he could talk up his limo company and get some business.

For the grand opening party they would have live music and three food trucks on the street. They had received news coverage on Saturday, so Joel was sure that the party Monday was going to be epic.

He hadn't seen too much of Kennedy, except when she helped

out and when he woke up each morning. It hadn't gone unnoticed that boxes kept multiplying in his house, and his neat and tidy house didn't resemble his home at all. But that was exactly what he'd wanted. It had been his idea for her to move in before they could actually allot the time for it.

As he'd moved through their bedroom that morning, he'd seen the outfit Kennedy was planning to wear when she arrived. It was a beautiful sundress with some strappy shoes. He had to assume that the flat shoes that were next to the strappy ones were her emergency shoes that would stay in the car or something. He loved that she planned out her outfits. For some reason knowing what she was going to wear and then seeing her in it gave him a jolt.

The afternoon of the grand opening party wasn't any different. The moment he saw Kennedy walk through the door in the sundress he'd seen on the hanger, his heart rate expedited and his palms grew damp. This was the woman he was going to marry and spend his entire life with, and every time he saw her he nearly burst.

"You look beautiful," he said as he rounded the bar and kissed her. "I couldn't wait to see that on you."

"Thank you. You look nice," she drew out the word and looked him over in his jeans, boots, and T-shirt with the tap house logo.

"It's a new trend. Everyone wants to look like this," he joked as he pointed to her brother behind the bar.

"You're sure you want him back there?"

"He's amazing. His people skills are fantastic."

Kennedy blew out a breath. "I'll take your word for it because I can't imagine."

They walked toward the bar and Chase leaned in on his elbows. "What do you think, sis? My kind of gig?"

"How many phone numbers do you have already?"

"*Moi?*" Chase put his hand in his pocket and pulled out eight scraps of paper. "Oh, the night is young," he grinned as he put the paper back in his pocket. "What can I pour you?"

"Something light."

Chase nodded and poured her a drink from the tap.

She took it as more people approached the bar. Joel slipped his arm around her waist. "My parents are by the jukebox. Do you want to sit with them?"

"That would be nice."

Joel escorted Kennedy to the table where his parents sat. His mother inching over to hug Kennedy and examine the ring again, even though she'd seen it a dozen times.

"I'm going to go check on the trucks," Joel said and Kennedy nodded as he headed outside.

June patted Kennedy's hand. "This crowd is three times bigger than the first opening they did. I think they're on to something here," she boasted. "I'm so proud of them."

"They've worked hard."

"I think they have a lot more people since the news did that story on them. I've seen a few people that I know he invited personally."

Kennedy sipped on her beer and watched as people came and went. Her brother managed the line at the bar with ease, and Joel worked the crowd as he walked back inside.

It was then she saw his eyes light up as a woman walked into the building and ran right for him, flinging her arms around his neck, and Joel spun her around. She introduced him to a man that followed her, but the smile on his face was wide and Kennedy wondered who the woman could be.

June noticed her as well. "Oh my goodness. Audrey is here," she said as she nudged Tim's arm and stood to greet the woman before they ever made it to the table.

Obviously this was a family member Kennedy hadn't met yet. Surely there would be a lot of these.

As they approached her, Kennedy stood, so she could meet the guests, but it was the look on Joel's face that said one of them was out of place. He certainly was happy enough to see the woman walking into his business, but he looked absolutely panic-stricken when they'd approached the table.

"Kennedy," June took her hand. "This is Audrey and her husband Douglas. This is Kennedy, Joel's fiancée."

"Fiancée?" Audrey's voice rose, and there was a flash of something before the smile returned. "That's fantastic. Congratulations."

"Thank you," Kennedy said as Joel's arm slipped around her waist.

"I didn't think you had it in you," Audrey teased and Joel chuckled. But his body had stiffened and now Kennedy had to know who this woman and her husband were.

"I'll get you two some drinks," Joel offered.

"We'll go up with you. This place is so amazing," Audrey said as she looped her arms through Joel's and her husband's and walked away.

Kennedy tried to ease back in her seat, but her hands shook when she picked up her beer. Why had that woman set her off like that?

"We haven't seen Audrey in, gosh, ten years," she said as she settled back in her seat. "She and Doug just got back from a mission trip in Africa. They've been there for nearly five years. She was always such a motivated girl, but her passion was globally not locally. They just couldn't make it work out, so she went her way, and he went his."

"Audrey and Doug?" Kennedy confirmed.

"Oh, no. I'm sorry. Audrey and Joel. Audrey is Joel's ex-wife."

CHAPTER 42

*J*oel introduced Audrey and Doug to Chase who ran through the beer list with them and set them up with some testers. When he looked back at the table where his parents sat, he noticed that Kennedy wasn't there.

He scanned the room, but she didn't stand out, and she would have stood out to him.

Excusing himself from those at the bar he walked back to the table. "Where did Kennedy go?"

His parents exchanged looks. "I don't know. She excused herself and got up."

"Shit."

His mother reached for his hand. "You did mention Audrey to her before, didn't you?"

Joel ran his hand over the stubbled beard on his chin. "The topic never came up."

"I'm sorry, dear. I told her who she was."

He knew that without the confirmation. Now he just needed to find Kennedy and straighten the whole thing out.

Joel headed for the back door, but before he could exit, he was stopped by three others who extended their congratulations. By the time he stepped through the back door, he watched as her car pulled away.

What was supposed to be one of the most magnificent nights of his life had just taken a drastic turn for the worse. Just because he didn't see that having an ex-wife was a big deal didn't mean it wasn't one to the woman who hadn't known. He should have cleared that up months ago. Hell, when they were taking about telling others that they loved them, and he'd admitted to having done so, that would have been the opportune time to mention the ex-wife.

"Hey, Joel." He looked up to see his brother coming toward him. "They need that saison tapped. Can you handle that? Oh, and did you see Audrey was here?"

Before he could tell Jeff that he'd have to handle the issue, he'd disappeared into the crowd. Dealing with Kennedy would have to wait.

KENNEDY'S HOUSE seemed eerily empty, but she'd be damned if she went back to his house. He'd be looking for her there first.

How dare he not tell her he'd been married before. Wouldn't that be something that should have been cleared early on? Seriously how did he miss that?

Kennedy threw her purse on the sofa and fell down next to it, her strappy sandals still stuck to her feet because she just didn't have the energy to untie them.

She winced when she heard her phone buzzing in her purse.

Please come back to the party. Let's talk. I love you.

She couldn't help it, she threw the phone across the room and didn't care to stand up and find it. What she needed was to be missing for a few hours. Tears needed to flow, words needed to be screamed, and pity needed to be felt. Everything she'd been so excited about was now just a pile of rubble as far as she was concerned. There was no way she was marrying a man who forgot to mention something as big as a marriage. Hell, where would he be the next time he forgot to mention it to someone? Only, if she went through with it, that marriage would be her marriage.

That was when the tears started. Breath came in pants, and relief came from curling up on her sofa and pulling the afghan off the back of the sofa and over her shoulders. Eventually she stopped hearing the buzzing of the phone that was on the floor across the room. Sleep took over, and she forgot about what waited for her when she left the comforts of her house.

There was no choice but to go back to life as normal the next day. Albeit she'd be doing it without a fresh manicure, thanks to the holiday. At some point she knew that Joel would invade her space, and he'd want to talk, but it was within her rights to tell him to leave. She'd give him back his ring, and they could just say it was a mistake. Lots of people made mistakes. At least they wouldn't have gone through with it.

Luckily, by the end of the week, she'd be headed to New York. Maybe she'd just extend her trip. No one could argue that she didn't deserve some time away.

Kennedy climbed out of her car quickly and hurried through the back door of the shop making sure to lock it so no one would follow her inside.

She dropped her purse off at her desk and walked to the front, nearly screaming when she noticed a man's body propped up against the door. At first, she thought a homeless man had fallen asleep, but this man had on the same clothes Joel had had on the night before, so that was too much of a coincidence.

Kennedy unlocked the door and flung it opened, tumbling Joel inside and waking him up.

"What in the hell are you doing?" she let her voice rise in pitch and volume.

Joel rubbed the side of his head before managing to his feet. "You weren't home last night, or this morning when I got home. I knew you'd be here, eventually."

"Well I'm here, now you should go."

He shook his head. "I'm not leaving until we talk."

"I don't have anything nice to say to you," she spat out the words and crossed her arms in front of her. "As far as I'm concerned…"

"I'll let you finish that thought later. I owe you an apology and I'm going to give it to you."

"You owe me more than that."

"An explanation, maybe? It's not like I'm still married to her. I didn't lie. I didn't cheat. I didn't mean for any of this to happen." He raked his fingers through his hair. "Damnit, Kennedy. I love you, and I'm not going down without a fight."

"A fight is what you're going to get."

"I deserve that." He shut the door to the store. "Let's go somewhere where we can sit down and discuss this."

"Hillary will be here in fifteen minutes and my first client will be here at nine. I still have a life to deal with."

Joel reached for her hand, but she pulled back. She wasn't ready for him to touch her. "I'm sorry. I'll say it a million more times, but I owe you an explanation. We need to talk about this."

"You should have disclosed this information at the start. How do you just forget that you have an ex-wife?"

"When I haven't been married to her for fifteen years, and wasn't married to her hardly at all. If you'd let me explain…"

They stopped talking as Hillary put her key in the lock and opened the door. She jumped when she saw them.

"I didn't see you guys standing there," she said as she pulled the headphones from her ears. "I'm listening to that Rob Lowe podcast and it's freaking amazing." She dropped her keys in her purse and then looked up at them. "Did I interrupt something?"

Kennedy shook her head. "No, I think we're done here," and with that she walked to the break room, made herself a cup of coffee, and waited to see Joel walk back to the building next door where he belonged.

When she saw him cross the lot, he looked up at the window where she stood. There was some satisfaction in turning her back on him.

CHAPTER 43

"I did walk in on something big. What the hell is going on, Ken?" Hillary leaned against the doorjamb.

Kennedy swiped the tear that was threatening to fall. "He was married. Just out of the blue some woman walks into the tap house last night, everyone jumps up to see her and hug her, oh, and by the way, it's Joel's ex-wife and her husband."

Hillary let out a long breath. "Whoa."

"Yeah, whoa." Kennedy dumped out the full cup of coffee she'd been holding and set the cup in the sink without washing it. "I don't need this. I don't need him. I was fine without him."

"Were you?"

"Oh, you're on his side?"

Hillary shrugged. "It did appear as if he were here to discuss it. I'm on team Joel, if you want my opinion, you should hear his side."

"I'm not in the mood for discussions. We should have had this discussion a long time ago."

"Or maybe you didn't have this discussion because it wasn't important."

Kennedy narrowed her stare at Hillary, who held up her hand to ward off Kennedy's attack.

"Hear me out." Hillary moved toward the table, pulled out a chair, and sat down. "Not everyone gets married for life. Maybe they were young. Maybe it was a fling. Maybe it was one of those childhood crushes that run off and get married. Do you know?"

Kennedy gritted her teeth. "No."

"Maybe she needed a visa to be in the country. Maybe she was dying of some disease she recovered from. Hell, maybe she got pregnant, but they didn't have the baby."

"That doesn't help."

"I'm saying there are a million reasons someone gets married and it's not important. Now, let's flip that. There are a million reasons, that in less than three months a man would propose to a woman with a pink stoned ring given to her in a box he made his mother when he was seven."

"That's a ploy."

"Sure as hell is. It's a ploy to get the woman that he loves to marry him. You said yes, Ken. You owe him the courtesy of a few minutes to explain himself."

"I don't owe him anything."

"You do. At some point in your prissy little life, you've done something you're not proud of but you've forgotten about at this moment. Somewhere, it'll come back to you and you'll have to explain yourself. And if he's as shallow as you, he'll walk away from you."

There were times when having a best friend was overrated, and this was one of those times, Kennedy decided. She didn't want to give him that moment. He didn't deserve it.

Luckily, the front door chimes alerted her that her client had arrived, and there was no need for Hillary to hold her hostage in the break room any longer. Kennedy skirted past her and went on with her day, now refusing to talk to both Joel and Hillary.

"I THINK that Kennedy's brother should give up driving those limos and come work for us," Jeff said as he walked into the small office where Joel had been hiding out. "We killed it last night when he was behind the bar. It's not like we're pouring shots and mixers. But he's got some charm." He tossed the report on the desk. "Look at those numbers."

"That's nice," Joel groaned without looking.

"You look like shit."

"I slept in a doorway."

"You have a house. Homelessness doesn't suit you." Jeff leaned in on his elbows. "So why exactly did you sleep in a doorway?"

Joel leaned back in his chair and raked his fingers through his hair. "Because my fiancée was unaware that I had an ex-wife. And said ex-wife happened to show up here."

Jeff winced. "I never thought about it when I sent her the invitation."

"I wouldn't have either," Joel admitted as he sat forward and rested his arms on the desk, mimicking his brother's. "Truth is, I didn't even think about Audrey. I don't think about her. It was a long time ago. It was a short period of time. I don't count it."

"But Kennedy does?"

"Because she won't let me talk to her. She's going to have to at some point. I mean, her entire house is scattered in my house in boxes. Whether she unpacks them there or comes and takes them away, she's going to have to talk to me."

"Man, I'm sorry."

"Don't be. When Audrey was around she was part of the family. She was part of the family as long as I can remember. Why wouldn't we ask her to celebrate with us? Doug is like a brother to both of us. I was as much a stone in her path as she was one in mine. Stumble over it. Get back up."

Jeff eased back in his seat. "I can talk to Kennedy. Hell, mom can talk to her. She'll never turn mom away."

The thought humored Joel, but he shook his head. "She leaves on Thursday for New York. Maybe when she gets back she'll be ready to talk."

"Or she'll have had enough time to work up a real good argument to throw that pink ring in your face."

"Either way, I deserve it."

Joel stood, shaking his head. "No, you don't deserve it. She'll come around. At least enough to hear you out."

"I hope so. Because if she doesn't, I'll use all the forces I have to make her listen. I might not have known her as long as I knew Audrey, but I feel so much more for her. What Kennedy and I have isn't some summer romance ending in a wedding. This is forever, man."

Jeff chuckled as he moved to the door. "You're preaching to the choir. I found mine, remember. I knew the minute I saw Dina she was it. You were a goner the second Kennedy showed up in all that pink and smelling so pretty."

"And I thought you didn't like her."

"I cast judgement too fast. She's a keeper, Joel. Don't give up. If she goes to New York first, use that time wisely, my friend, to plan for her return. She's your one. I know it."

Joel watched his brother walk away. He was right, she was his one. How in the hell was he ever going to convince her to listen to him?

CHAPTER 44

For the first time since she'd opened, Kennedy had another first. Sickness nor family crisis had ever made Kennedy cancel or rearrange appointments, but she'd done it.

With half of her house at Joel's and the other half scattered around her own house, there was nowhere she was comfortable being. She needed to get out of town, so why not head to New York early?

Without even telling Hillary her plans, she changed her airline tickets and her hotel room. She rescheduled her clients and left Hillary a detailed note as to what she'd done. Then she called her sister for a ride to the airport.

"Don't you think you should have called Dad?" Paige asked as she maneuvered her way through traffic in her vintage VW Beetle. "Seriously, he owes you more of these favors than I do."

"I could have rented a limo to take me, too, but I chose you so you could mouth me," she snapped back. "I'll pay you. Or whatever, just get me there."

"Nice to see you'll be flying into NYC with an NYC attitude."

"I deserve this attitude."

"Bullshit," her sister spat out the words. "You're being petty. But heck, suck up the drama. It's not like he ruined your life. But why not ruin the most perfect thing to ever happen to you by being stubborn. The Kennedy Devereaux way."

"I didn't ask you for a ride so you could berate me."

"I think you did. I think you need someone to tell you exactly what kind of ass you're being."

Luckily that bit of news came as they pulled up to the airport and Kennedy swiftly opened her door. "Don't bother to pick me up when I get back. I don't need your counsel," she argued as she pulled her suitcase out from behind her seat.

"What you need is a shrink," Paige hollered as Kennedy kicked the door closed and headed into the terminal.

JOEL CAREFULLY OPENED the pink door that led to Kennedy's store. The dozen roses and baby's breath rustled as he stepped over the threshold. No one was behind the counter. A moment later Hillary walked out from the back and put her hands on her hips.

"Groveling with roses?" she asked.

"I'll grovel with whatever works."

"Well, you've wasted your money," she informed him as she walked around the counter. "She's gone. I came to work, and she'd left me a long note. She cancelled her clients and left town."

Joel dropped his arms and the flowers now faced the floor. "She left town?"

Hillary hurried around the counter and took the bouquet from him. "Yes, but don't ruin these. You had to have spent a hundred dollars on these." She carried them to the break room and Joel followed. She opened a cabinet full of vases and took one down. "She didn't tell me where she was going. She just said she needed to leave. I know she'll be in New York by the end of the week, but right now I don't know where she is."

"Did you call her?"

Hillary shot him a look over her shoulder as she filled the vase with water. "Called. Texted. Emailed. Facebook Messenger. Instagram message. Tweeted. LinkedIn message and Snapchatted. Yes, I called."

Joel wiped the back of his hand over his forehead. "Well, that's that."

The chime over the door rang and then the door slammed. They both turned to see Paige hurtling toward the break room.

"No doubt you're both in here crying over Kennedy missing."

Hillary placed the roses in the vase. "You know where she is?"

"Keeper of all the knowledge. And I'm going to give it to you. She's in a foul mood. She's bossy. She's snotty, and she needs to be knocked to the ground."

Hillary snorted out a laugh, but Joel moved to Paige in desperation. "Okay, where is she?"

"You did a job on her."

"I didn't do anything. I left out a little information on my past, but it was unintentional."

"Is that why she's your ex? You forgot you had her?"

That was a low blow, but he deserved that. "She's my ex because things in our lives didn't align."

"I'll give you the information, but you tell me the whole story before you run out of here. And I want a shift at your tap house. I have a new business opportunity and I need some extra money."

For the first time in days, Joel laughed. "You're hired. Just tell Jeff when to put you on the schedule. Now where is she?"

"She left for New York early." Paige pulled a piece of paper from her pocket and handed it to him. "She registered the room under my name, since no one was looking for me. Originally she was going to stay at the Plaza, but she moved hotels. Now she's at the Marriott in Times Square. And, because she's registered under my name, I called and added you to the room."

His heart felt lighter than it had in days. "So I can check in and get a key?"

"Genius, huh? If she calls the cops, you'll get arrested in New York."

"It's so worth it. I love her. You both know I didn't mean any harm. She'd know that if she'd just listen to me."

Both women looked at him, their arms crossed in front of them.

Paige narrowed her eyes. "You do realize we know what kind of drama queen she is and that's why I'm giving you this bit of information. I love my sister, but she's built her life on a little bit of drama. Thank my father for that. But if you can corner her, you can tell her your story. I can't guarantee she'll listen, but…"

"But what could it hurt, huh?" Joel clutched the piece of paper to his chest. "Thank you, Paige. I owe you."

"You just gave me a job and you might piss my sister off. We're even. Now you owe me a story."

CHAPTER 45

Kennedy flipped through the channels on the television. She hadn't slept well, and she wished she had. Though she was used to traveling on her own, it was usually for business. Without business to attend to, she didn't know what to do with herself. There was also the fact that her phone and iPad were off so that no one could bother her. Surely everyone had tried, and she'd have been disappointed if Joel hadn't, even if she didn't want to talk to him.

She'd ordered breakfast and thrown on a pair of shorts and a T-shirt. Her hair was piled on top of her head, and she'd pulled the sheets up on the bed just to appear a little more organized than she felt. The truth was she was a mess, and she wasn't used to being so emotional.

The curtains were open and the city buzzed to life below her. There was some appeal to getting lost in a city, she thought, as she stood by the window, but then again, she rather enjoyed knowing *Kennedy Devereaux Designs* was a big deal in her mid-sized town.

When there was a knock at the door, she stood.

"Room service," the voice on the other side said.

Just at the mention of it, her stomach growled.

She opened the door and the man in his hotel uniform pushed the cart inside the room. "Would you like it set by the window?" he asked, his accent thick but indecipherable.

"Yes, please."

The man made quick work of setting it up and hurried back to the door. "Already signed for. Good day."

Kennedy looked at the tray and then at the man who quickly walked away. "Wait, this is the wrong tray. There are two settings. I only ordered one."

It was then that the movement from across the hall caught her eye and Joel walked toward her.

"Paige Devereaux?"

How the hell did he know she'd done that? That was a stupid question to even contemplate. Of course her sister was in on this.

"This isn't funny. I specifically left early so I didn't have to deal with anyone. Why are you here?"

"I have a key. Would you rather I use it? You can call the front desk and ask, but I'm assigned to this room. Paige called and set it up. And I've been traveling all night. I could use that breakfast I ordered."

Anger filled her body with heat and rage, but she wasn't sure if she should aim it at her ex-fiancé or her sister. Then again, she wanted to weep and fall into Joel's arms because she knew she was just being stubborn, and she loved him. But there was a something bigger happening here, and she wasn't going to back down.

"I didn't invite you."

He shook his head. "You certainly didn't. It would have been nice. I'll get to see Paris though," he said with a wink and the heat in her body from anger rose.

"You're certainly not going to Paris now."

"You've written me off completely?"

Kennedy held up her bare finger. "Yes."

"That's too bad. But with me here, we can talk without any interruptions."

Joel slid past her and into the room carrying a suitcase. Did he really think she was going to let him stay? Was she going to let him stay?

Kennedy closed the door and watched as the man who made her heart rate rise set his suitcase down. He was dressed in jeans and a T-shirt, and the beard growth was nearly filled in. It was appealing she thought, but she was still mad as hell.

He lifted the domes off of the plates. "Belgian waffle. Just what I wanted."

"Maybe you could eat it in the hallway."

"Nope," he said as he pulled a piece of bacon from her plate and took a bite. "Your eggs are getting cold."

"What are you doing in New York? I came out early so I didn't have to see you."

Joel sat down in the chair nearest his waffle and began to spread butter on it. "See, I would be thinking *Oh, he has something to say*. You think I'm stalking you."

"I didn't say that."

"But you don't want to hear what I have to say?"

"Telling me you're sorry isn't going to make this go away."

Joel cut a piece of the waffle and shoved it into his mouth, then held up a finger to hold her off until he swallowed, and sipped from his water glass. "You're right. In fact, I'm not even going to use the word sorry, because mostly, I'm not sorry. I'm going to sit here, in your hotel room in New York, and tell you all about Audrey."

Kennedy bit down on her bottom lip. When he said her name out loud it caused her heart to ache even more. "I don't want to know anything about her."

"You might. She's an amazing woman."

The words stung since they flew so freely from his lips. "Your mother made her sound like a saint."

Joel nodded and took another bite of his waffle. "If she were a religious figure, yeah, she might get sainted someday. The world is a much better place because of her."

"So then why would she divorce you? Wouldn't a saint stick around and fix whatever was wrong?"

"A saint would. A sinner would walk. You should come eat your breakfast and listen, because I'm not leaving. I love you. I still have all intentions of marrying you. This is a bump in our road. We haven't really had one of those yet."

She was hungry, and he still affected her in a way that she couldn't just ignore him. His hair was begging for her to tunnel her fingers through it. And that beard—it really was sexy.

Kennedy walked across the room and sat down in the opposite chair. She took a slice of bacon from her plate and bit off a piece.

"Okay, sinner. Tell me why you walked."

a smile settled on Joel's lips as he uncovered the cups of coffee and took a sip from his cup. "I met Audrey when I was six years old. She lived across the street from us. I would figure her to be a lot like you. Pigtails done up in ribbon and pretty dresses, but she liked to play tough. Her knees had bandages on them all the time and those dresses were dirty, though they hadn't started that way. If they'd let women play freaking football, she'd have been a professional kicker. I kid you not. Soccer scholarships and full rides to huge colleges. Lost her virginity in the back of a truck under the stars by the lake to a loser who would only go to tech school to learn how to wire electricity."

"You're no loser," she said in a near whisper.

"Didn't say I was the loser, did I?"

Kennedy hunched her shoulders, feeling mighty small for the assumption.

Joel took another sip of his coffee. "She'd moved away when we were thirteen, but we'd ended up at the same high school. We went to homecoming and prom together our senior year. I knew every secret she ever kept, and she knew all of mine. Anyway, she got those full rides to college and went away. I'd go visit on vacations, but by then we weren't really a couple. Then she hooked back up with the loser. Hot and heavy romance. Her parents didn't approve and threatened to stop paying her expenses if she kept seeing him. Little white lie, she told them we were dating."

"And you went along with it?"

He shrugged. "What would it hurt? They didn't live across the street anymore, and if she came around once in a while, my parents were all for it. My mom adored her."

"Fake boyfriend."

"Fake boyfriend. She kept seeing the loser, and it got to the point even I was trying to talk her into breaking up with him, to no avail. Then came the night she was standing at my door crying. I took her in and she slept in my bed. The next morning she told me why she was there. She was pregnant and when she'd told the loser, he took off."

"Total loser," Kennedy picked up the other piece of bacon and nibbled on it.

"If she told her parents they wouldn't pay her expenses or tuition, and being pregnant she was going to lose her scholarships. She was going to be a social worker, and damn, she's a good one."

"So you married her?"

"I loved her. She was one of my dearest friends, and we'd dated, so we meant something to one another. Her parents liked me and my parents loved her. A baby wasn't convenient, but with me, it wasn't the end of the world. No one had to threaten her or the baby because they trusted me. The baby was due in the summer, and it was the most opportune time for it. In theory, we'd have the baby during break. We got married at Christmas. The ceremony was tiny. My parents. Her parents. My brother and Dina. Her sister. I would never have let her go through it on her own."

Kennedy picked up her water and took a long sip. There was a knot in her throat, and she had to swallow it down before it became a flood of tears. "You don't have a baby."

He shook his head. "I don't have a baby. She lost the baby in the second trimester. Spontaneous. She was healthy, but it just happened."

The tears began anyways. Kennedy reached her hand across the table and took his. "I'm sorry."

"Six months. We were married for six months. After graduation we got a quick divorce. She stayed a close friend, met Douglas, and off they went on worldly adventures to fix the world. It's exactly what she'd always wanted to do. I started working in an accounting firm, hated it, and started flipping houses with my brother shortly after."

"And no one ever knew the baby was the loser's?"

"My parents knew. They knew everything. Her parents think our marriage fell apart because of the baby. It saves face for her. I don't mind. The point is, I didn't mention it because I don't count it. I don't even remember it most times. It wasn't real in my head, but it was," he admitted. "I loved Audrey and she loved me. But now I love you and she loves Douglas. Once in a while she shows up, and she gets the reception she got at the party. Never would I have thought to explain it to you until she came around. She's not part of my life now and hasn't been for a very, very long time."

"And you're not sorry for all of that?"

"I'm sorry I don't see her more often. She has some amazing stories of the places of the world she and Doug have lived. The wells they've dug for villages. The vaccinations they've given to children that might have died without them." He shook his head again. "I'm not sorry for any of it. I'm only sorry you found out the way you did."

And now she had to decide what she was going to do with all of the information he'd just given her. Seriously, in a story of sinners and saints, he came out as the saint in her book.

"I should have asked a few more questions," Kennedy

admitted as she picked up a piece of toast and smeared grape jelly on it. "Your mother probably thinks I'm a sore loser."

"My mother loves you. She's a bit miffed that she was the one that let the cat out of the bag, and that I hadn't let it out of the bag already. But in your position, I don't think anyone would blame you for being angry."

"Petty. Angry is one thing. Being petty is another. It cost me the screen on my phone, three days of work, and I took off my engagement ring and left it in my office. I was going to give it back to you because I was trying convince myself that I hated you."

"You don't?"

Kennedy set down her toast and folded her hands in her lap. "I don't hate you, and I think that's why I'm sitting here feeling like an idiot. Audrey was lucky to have you. I'm lucky to have you."

"I still want to marry you. Having a baby with Audrey wasn't in the plans. But I hope you'll consider having one with me. Seeing you with Cara's daughter, well, it choked me up."

A laugh escaped Kennedy, and she pressed her fingers to her lips. "I'd never considered children until I looked at you holding her daughter. You're a natural."

Joel stood and walked around the little table, kneeling down in front of Kennedy and taking her hand. "Are we good here?"

His eyes were soft, and his voice so even, how could she ever have thought she was so mad at him that she could walk away from him?

"We're good."

"Good," he sighed as he put his hand into the front pocket of his jeans and pulled out her ring. "Now, let's put this back on."

The tears that had been wavering all morning rolled down Kennedy's cheeks. "You brought my ring? You found my ring?"

"It was on your desk in that little tea cup where you put your jewelry when you're working on your computer. Your sister used your computer to get all the information set up for my trip."

Kennedy pulled Joel to her and laughed softly in his ear. "I owe her one."

"She's paid up. She asked for a job."

Kennedy eased back. "A job? She has a job."

"She needs some capital to buy a yoga studio," he said before he pressed his lips to hers. "I want to make you a promise. I will never hurt you on purpose. There are still stories you might never have heard, we're kinda fresh into this relationship even if we're moving into a forever position. But I'm not hiding anything from you, so if you get mad, you have to tell me."

Kennedy pressed her forehead to his. "I promise. I don't like being mad at you. It makes me look bad."

"Oh, and you could never look bad. You are hands down the most put-together, sexiest woman I have ever met. I didn't know pink could be as unique as a signature."

"Wait until you see the wedding dress I'm designing."

"Pink?"

"You can't go wrong with pink. Especially *Kennedy Pink*."

Joel scooped her out of the chair and carried her to the bed. He gently laid her down and moved in next to her to kiss her. "I cannot wait to see what you design. It was the pink on your doors that drew me to your shop."

"Is this where you pictured us that day?"

He brushed a strand of hair from her face and kissed her again. "The moment I smelled your perfume and turned to see your face, it was absolutely where I pictured us." He tugged at the hem of her shirt, lifting it over her head exposing her soft pink bra. "Pink. I will never tire of pink."

EPILOGUE

Snow had fallen overnight, and Kennedy wondered if their wedding guests would even make it to the wedding. They hadn't planned a huge wedding, but when she started making their guest list, she realized they just knew a lot of people that they considered important. Cara sat in the corner of the dressing room in the back of Kennedy's store with her feet up on the ottoman, her pink bridesmaid dress altered to fit her body. After all those years of trying for a baby and finally getting one, now she was pregnant with twins. Kennedy knew that she was overjoyed at the blessing, even though she looked absolutely miserable.

Dina applied her mascara in one of the small mirrors they'd brought in for makeup.

Hillary turned from the small cart in the room with two glass of champagne. She handed one to Kennedy and then one to Dina.

"We need to toast." She handed a glass filled with apple juice to Cara. "Don't you move. Just sit there."

Cara smiled up at her. "You don't have to tell me twice."

Picking up the last glass of champagne on the cart, she turned to the center of the room. "To our Kennedy. Oh, I never, ever thought this day would come for you."

"Hey," Kennedy whined.

"Seriously. At what point were you ever going to leave your store to find a man? How interesting it was that the store brought him to you. So here's to you and that cute guy next door in the work boots and T-shirt that you weren't obsessively staring at through the break room window."

Kennedy laughed. "To him."

Cara lifted her glass. "To both of you."

The door to the room opened and Kennedy's father walked into the room. "I think they're ready for you," he said.

Kennedy set the glass of champagne on the cart, untouched. Hillary helped Cara to her feet and with Dina they walked out of the room. A moment later, Kennedy heard the chimes above the door sound, and she knew they'd walked next door.

"Are you sure you want to do this?" her father asked.

"Why wouldn't I? I love him."

"I wouldn't have done my job if I didn't ask. He's a wonderful man. I'm proud to call him my son," he said and Kennedy had to bat back the tears that threatened her makeup.

"He is a wonderful man. I'm ready now."

She took her father's arm and left the pink hue of her store and stepped out into the sparkling snow to walk next door to marry the man who had changed her life.

The tap house was nearly unrecognizable, Joel thought. It was draped in white and pink. The tables and stools had been replaced with white chairs, and in those chairs sat the people that meant the most to them. Next to him stood his brother and his future brothers-in-law. His mother was already crying, and he found that humorous. It wasn't as if she hadn't seen her sons get married. But he knew this one was different. Kennedy's mother held her step-father's hand and Joel was sure she kept dabbing the handkerchief to her eyes, under the large brim of her hat.

Four rows back, Audrey rested her hands pregnant stomach while Doug kept his arm around her shoulders. Joel's life with her seemed so long ago, and now here she was, sitting at his wedding and shedding tears he knew were joyous. It had been Kennedy's idea to invite them. She'd even taken Audrey to lunch to give her the invitation. When she'd returned, she'd had a new respect for the woman who was changing the world, and had once used Joel as a fake boyfriend.

When he saw the women in their pink dresses walk through the door, he knew it was time. His heart began to beat faster and his palms grew damp. The guitarist they'd hired for the ceremony began to play and Dina started down the aisle. She waved at her daughter who was on her knees in her chair blowing kisses at her mother.

Cara walked down the aisle slowly. She smiled at her husband as she took her place at the front.

When Hillary started down the aisle, her auburn hair piled atop her head and ringlets framing her face, Joel heard the sounds that came from behind him.

"Dear Lord, she's amazing."

When he gave the slightest glance over his shoulder he noticed that Jeff and Max had turned to Chase, whose eyes were fixed on the woman walking toward them.

Was Joel imagining things? Were her eyes fixed on Chase too?

None of that mattered. A moment later when the guests stood, he got his first glimpse of his bride. Her veil and tiara accented the blonde curls, and her eyes sparkled when she looked at him. The dress was white, and that surprised him, but then he noticed the very subtle trim, which was *Kennedy Pink*. Each bouquet had had pink flowers, but just like the dress, her bouquet had white roses and pink rose accents.

The details baffled him, and he wondered why he even had

noticed them. Because they'd been painstakingly chosen by the love of his life. Kennedy Devereaux. The woman with the signature pink doors that had drawn him to look inside.

When she reached him, her father kissed her cheek and then sat next to Kennedy's mother and step-father.

"I didn't imagine you could look more beautiful than you usually do. I swear you're glowing."

Kennedy's eyes lowered and lifted again. "There's a reason for that."

"Why's that?"

She looked at the guests and then back at him. Lifting on her toes she leaned in.

"I'm pregnant," she whispered in his ear.

He felt the blood drain from his face. "Seriously?"

"I wouldn't make that up right here," she said softly.

"You're pregnant?" he repeated what she'd whispered, only when he said it, it wasn't whispered.

Jeff's hand came down on his shoulder. "Dude, congratulations, but maybe have that conversation elsewhere?"

Joel chuckled as he looked at his mother whose fingertips were pressed to her lips, concealing her knowing smile.

"This day is only getting better," he said. "Let's get this over with. Wow," he let out a breath. "A baby."

"The minister leaned in. Does this mean you take this man to be your husband?" he asked the question directed to Kennedy.

She laughed. "Of course I do."

"Joel? Do you take…"

"God, yes I do," he blurted out before he cupped her face and pulled her in for a kiss.

"I take you as my wife and the mother of my children." He turned to the guests. "We're having a baby, too."

He pulled Kennedy to him. They were two people who did things with their own set of rules. Why should their wedding day be any different?

"I love you," she said, as he pulled her in even closer.

"I love you, too, and you did an amazing job with your gown."

He sighed as he kissed her again.

Joel turned to the minister. "Sorry to have interrupted. Go ahead. Start wherever you'd like. I'm ready to take my bride now."

MEET THE AUTHOR

Bestselling Author Bernadette Marie is known for building families readers want to be part of. Her series The Keller Family has graced bestseller charts since its release in 2011. Since then she has authored and published over forty books. The married mother of five sons promises romances with a *Happily Ever After always*...and says she can write it because she lives it.

Obsessed with the art of writing and the business of publishing, chronic entrepreneur Bernadette Marie established her own publishing house, 5 Prince Publishing, in 2011 to bring her own work to market as well as offer an opportunity for fresh voices in fiction to find a home as well. Bernadette is also an educator in the industry, offering workshops and speaking at conferences. In 2020 she was named the Independent Writer of the Year from the Rocky Mountain Fiction Writers.

When not immersed in the writing/publishing world, Bernadette Marie and her husband are shuffling their five hockey playing boys around town to practices and games as well as running their family business. She is a lover of a good stout craft beer and might be slightly addicted to chocolate.

We hope you enjoyed book one in the Devereaux Family Series, *Kennedy Devereaux.* Please enjoy an excerpt from book two, *Chase Devereaux.*

CHASE DEVEREAUX

CHAPTER 1

*S*un. Why in the hell did it have to be so bright?

Chase lifted his arm and draped it over his face to shield his eyes. The only responsibility he had today was to take the Cadillac limo to pick up his sister and her husband and take them to the airport. He wouldn't have to leave until seven o'clock that night. With the sun blinding him, he knew it was much too early to be up.

He'd tied one on the night before at his sister's wedding. What did they expect? They'd had it at the tap house her husband owned. Of course, had he stuck to beer, he might have been okay. But they'd brought in other liquor since it was a private event, and he'd taken part in it. Boy had he.

There were some fuzzy spots in his memory when he thought about the night. One thing was for certain, he knew he hadn't driven home, but he wasn't sure how he got home.

Lifting his arm off his face, he opened one eye and looked around. Yep, this was his house, and his horribly decorated bedroom.

That smelly dog bed still sat in the corner, and that poor, old hound dog had crossed the rainbow bridge months ago. God, he missed that dog.

As he lowered his arm, someone turned in the bed next to him. Their arm came over his chest and he froze. It wasn't the first time he'd had a woman in his bed that he hadn't remembered bringing there. There were some unfortunate effects of alcohol. Sometimes he didn't remember bringing anyone home with him. Other times, he'd bring them home and not be able to perform and they'd both just pass out. There wasn't any pride in it, but then, he didn't feel guilty either.

He picked up the hand that rested on his chest and examined it. At least there wasn't a ring on the finger. He'd been known to find that from time to time. Though Chase liked to have fun, and a willing woman was just his cup of joe, he did believe in the sanctity of marriage for those who had ventured into it. Sleeping with someone's wife wasn't his thing.

Auburn hair splayed out over the pillow next to him, and the woman's face was turned the other direction.

But as she moved ever so slightly again, he saw the tell-tale sign and he knew exactly who he'd taken to bed with him.

Only one woman he knew of had a butterfly tattoo in watercolor on her left shoulder blade. He would always remember it because he'd gone with her when she'd gotten it. And somehow, she'd convinced him to get the same tattoo in the same place.

Over the years he'd convinced others that it was in memory of his grandmother who had passed when he was little. But that was just bullshit so no one would think he was some kind of sissy with a butterfly tattoo.

When she turned her head to the side and faced him, Chase watched as she opened her eyes—those emerald green eyes. At least she smiled next and didn't come up swinging.

She let out a sigh. "Well, crap. We ended up here again, didn't we?" Her voice was raspy from sleep.

"Looks like it."

"We're never going to hear the end of this."

"My sister leaves for her honeymoon in a few hours. If she saw us leave together, she'll have forgotten about it by the time she gets back."

"Then again, if she saw us, she would have stopped us."

That was true, he thought.

Hillary Mills rolled onto her back and pulled the sheet up to cover herself. Hillary, his sister's best friend and employee, had been in his bed more than this one time. A one-night stand years ago had stirred up enough trouble for them. They'd promised they'd never do it again, as it seemed to have upset his sister Kennedy quite a bit.

More than likely it was the looseness of morals surrounding the idea of a one-night stand that bothered Kennedy, and to think it had happened between her brother and best friend had been inconceivable for her. But that kind of crap happened all the time to Chase.

He knew the side of Hillary that was a party girl. And she knew his side. So as long as they didn't make this awkward, they could enjoy what had happened—as soon as they remembered it.

Hillary took his hand and interlaced their fingers, which he thought was a bit intimate. "When did you get the sporty car?" she asked.

"Is that what we drove home in?"

"Yep."

"I don't own a sporty car. You stole someone's ride, Hill."

She laughed that throaty laugh that always twisted him up inside. "Well, shit. I guess we're going to jail. You know what they do to sexy boys like you, don't you?"

Chase swallowed hard. Why was she being playful and intimate? Wasn't she freaked out by this too?

"I'm glad you think I'm sexy, but I don't even want to think about what they do to guys like me."

She laughed again and he had to close his eyes and will away the feelings that it stirred in him.

"I'm starving. What do you have to eat here?"

He gave it some thought. "Frozen burritos."

"Gross."

"That's what I have."

"Let's get dressed and go get breakfast. My treat."

Chase rubbed his eyes. "What time is it?"

Hillary rolled over, the sheets adjusting to give him a full view of her. "It's three o'clock in the afternoon."

"There's that burger place at the end of the block," he offered.

"Yeah, I could go for that."

They laid there a moment longer, as if neither of them were willing to stand up and expose themselves to the other one.

Finally, Hillary sat up on the edge of the bed. "Do you have something I can wear? I'm not putting on that dress again."

Chase looked across the room at the pink bridesmaid dress draped over a chair. "I don't know what would freak my sister out more; us in here naked together, or that dress in that condition."

"It's a toss-up."

"There are T-shirts in the closet, and I have some sweatpants in the drawer."

"This many clothes on the floor and you still have clothes put away?"

He wanted to make some stupid comment about keeping clean clothes put away for the women who need them, but he thought better of it. This was Hillary after all. She deserved more respect.

"Consider me only half a slob."

She stood and walked to the closet. Everything about her made everything about him react all at once.

Hillary pulled a shirt from a hanger and slid it over her body, pulling her hair out from under the collar and letting it cascade down her back. "I don't think you're a slob. Maybe it makes you the creative lover that you are," she complimented as she bent over to take a pair of sweatpants out of the drawer.

It was a shame that out of respect for his sister, there would never be anything between him and Hillary, because if she thought he was creative when he was drunk, she'd really appreciate him when he was sober.

Corporate Christmas *Bernadette Marie*
Faith Through Falling Snow *Sandy Sinnett*
After School Adventure: Beyond the Briar Patch *Antony Soehner*
Walker Defense Bernadette Marie
Clash of the Cheerleaders *April Marcom*
Stevie-Girl and the Phantom of Forever *Ann Swann*
Assemble the Party *Antony Soehner*
The Last Goodbye *Bernadette Marie*
The Gingerbread Curse *April Marcom*
Stevie-Girl and the Phantom of Crybaby Bridge *Ann Swann*
The MacBrides: Hannah & Ash *J.L. Petersen*
Leather and Lies *Celeste Straub*
Beginnings *Bernadette Marie*
Love and Loopholes *Railyn Stone*
Unite The Party *Antony Soehner*
Star Seer April Marcom
Totally Devoted *E.M. Bannock*
Bases Loaded *Jena James*
The Tea Shop *Bernadette Marie*
Walker Spirit *Bernadette Marie*
Remains in the Pond *Ann Swann*
Gather The Party *Antony Soehner*
Stevie-Girl and the Phantom Pilot *Ann Swann*
Chasing Shadows *Bernadette Marie*
The MacBrides: Logan and RJ *J.L. Petersen*
Never Saw It Coming *Bernadette Marie*
Blissful Disaster *Amy L. Gale*
Victory *Bernadette Marie*
Chasing Her Heart *J. L. Petersen*
Hope in the Rain *Sandy Sinnett*

www.ingramcontent.com/pod-product-compliance
Lightning Source LLC
Chambersburg PA
CBHW030404020726
47493CB00003B/941